Stranded and alone...
miles from home

Wandering through the hotel lobby Dina contemplated her predicament. Philippe, her fiancé, had sent her an urgent telegram asking her to join him. And now he had disappeared.

But he was not the type for false alarms. That was more the style of Eric, her ex-fiancé, the unfaithful and reckless man she had tried so long to forget.

Suddenly Eric's arrogant features appeared before her. What on earth was he doing in Tripoli? The answer was more complicated than Dina could have imagined.

And dangerous!

Rendezvous in Tripoli

by CAROLINE GAYET

Harlequin Books
NEW YORK • TORONTO

RENDEZVOUS IN TRIPOLI/first published December 1977

ISBN 0-373-90018-X

PRINTED IN CANADA

Chapter 1

"Ladies and gentlemen, in a few minutes...." The stewardess was repeating in English what she had just said in Italian. No other translation. I was the only French passenger on that flight from Rome to Tripoli. Luckily I knew both Italian and English well enough to understand that in a few minutes we would fly over Palermo.

I leaned toward the window. In the cloudless night, the lights of the city glittered like a crown of diamonds encircling a dark sea. Palermo, Sicily. We'd dreamed of going there....

I quickly caught myself before my thoughts went any further. My memory was playing tricks on me. It wasn't my fiancé, Philippe, who had planned to take me to Sicily; it was Eric, the man I'd broken off with two years earlier. I blamed my confusion on nervous tension, which had been made even worse

5

by the fatigue of traveling and my long wait at the Rome airport.

After leaving Paris at a quarter to twelve I had arrived in Italy at two in the afternoon. The plane to Tripoli wasn't scheduled to take off till five o'clock. I could have made a quick trip into Rome but I didn't feel like it. Instead, I wandered through the long, low-ceilinged buildings where all other sounds were regularly drowned out by the blare of announcements over the loudspeakers. I walked back and forth past the same shop windows filled with luggage, ties, umbrellas and dolls.

Jostled by the crowd of travelers from all countries and deafened by the noise, I finally took refuge in a cocktail lounge. There, in the semidarkness and relative quiet, I abandoned myself to the anxiety I hadn't been able to shake off.

Outside, it was a beautiful day. A stiff wind blew across the runways but the sun was shining and the temperature was springlike. I'd left an icy Paris wrapped in November mist. I wondered what the weather would be like in Tripoli.

Before leaving, I'd tried to find out what kind of clothes I'd need in Libya, but the contradictory opinions I'd received were confusing. Some of my friends had predicted overpowering heat; a man at the Libyan consulate had told me the weather would be about the same as in Paris.

I couldn't understand why Philippe hadn't written to tell me what to expect. Even though I'd had to get ready on short notice, he could have sent me a special-delivery letter. His telegram and the few words we'd exchanged on the telephone told me little.

My illogical feelings made me smile. I was annoyed with Philippe for not telling me what kind of clothes to bring, when I still didn't know the answer to a much more important question: why had he asked me to drop everything and come immediately to a strange country?

I reached into my purse, took out the telegram I'd received a week earlier and reread it:

I need you. Please come soon as possible. Tell me when and I will send plane ticket.
    Philippe

Under his name was an address: the Hotel Uaddan, Tripoli.

That urgent message seemed so unlike his usual way of doing things that I didn't hesitate a second in making up my mind to go. Since I worked in my father's law office, I had no trouble getting time off from my job. My parents were opposed to the idea at first but I stubbornly insisted that Philippe wouldn't have asked me to come if it wasn't very important, and that I couldn't let him down. They finally gave in, maybe because they realized I would go whether they approved or not. At twenty-two, I was a free agent.

My first thought was that Philippe might be
seriously ill. I called the Hotel Uaddan in Tripoli and
was told that he had gone away for several days.
The fact that he had left the hotel after sending the
telegram proved he wasn't sick. I couldn't imagine
why he wanted to see me so quickly, but I knew he
wasn't the kind of man to make such a request
without a serious reason.

I needed a Libyan visa, and to get it I had to show a
smallpox vaccination certificate. When I took the
certificate to the consulate, I was told it would take
four or five days for my visa to come through. I sent
Philippe a telegram saying I'd be ready to leave by
November seventh.

Three days later a messenger from a travel agency
brought me a first-class plane ticket. I was discon-
certed by the thought of traveling so luxuriously.
That wasn't like Philippe, either. My parents
regarded his extravagance as alarming and concluded that he must have lost his mind. To reassure
them, I tried to call him.

Two days before my departure, I succeeded in
getting him on the phone at his hotel. The connection was bad; his voice sounded strange and I could
barely hear him—not that it mattered much, since he
only repeated that he needed me and said he
couldn't explain it on the phone. I gave up trying to
find out anything more till I saw him again.

I was no better informed when I took off from
Paris. In other circumstances, the trip would have

interested me. Champagne and oysters are not tourist-class fare and once we were past the clouds that covered France I began to see some breathtaking scenes: the snowy Alps, the Gulf of Genoa, Corsica, Elba, and finally the Italian coast. The air was so clear that I could see each town, bay and mountain.

From Rome to Tripoli every seat in the plane was filled. As we flew over the Mediterranean the sun set in a blaze of spectacular colors and then darkness fell.

Now, AS WE APPROACHED the coast of Libya, the stars rent the dark heavens and surrounded a crescent moon.

I was still thinking about my mental slip confusing Philippe with Eric. I decided my mother must have been responsible for it. She'd driven me to the airport and, just before leaving, had told me that she would never have let me make such a trip if I'd been engaged to "that harebrained Eric Darnal" instead of to Philippe. I was surprised to hear that because it was the first time she'd mentioned Eric's name since my engagement.

But I had to admit to myself that I didn't need my mother to remind me of Eric's existence. I hadn't forgotten him. He was my first love and I knew how strongly my disappointment in him had affected my life. That experience was the cause of the long engagement I'd imposed on Philippe, and the

excuses I kept inventing for postponing our mar-
riage. Since I still hadn't completely recovered from
Eric's betrayal, I didn't want to marry Philippe until
I was absolutely sure of him, and of myself.

I knew I was being unfair; Philippe deserved my
trust. But I was obsessed by the thought that if it
hadn't been for my parents' opposition I would have
married Eric before I discovered his unfaithfulness.
My quick decision to go to Tripoli when Philippe
asked me to was greatly motivated by remorse.

Among other possible explanations for his request, I wondered if he'd finally lost patience and
decided to marry me away from the influence of our
families and friends. Such determination and
forcefulness would have impressed me, but I didn't
really believe it was true. To take such a romantic
initiative, he'd have had to change a great deal since
the last time I saw him.

I often wished he were less cautious and sensible;
yet his stability and common sense were among the
qualities I most appreciated in him. They reassured
me, especially since they were at the opposite pole
from the passionate, impulsive nature that made
Eric so attractive and so disappointing.

Chapter 2

We were making our final approach to Tripoli. The stewardess asked all the passengers to fasten their seat belts and put out their cigarettes. My heart began beating faster.

I knew very little about the country where I was about to land, even though Philippe had been working there for eight months. When the E.R.P.C., the oil company that employed him as an engineer, had told him that he was going to be sent to Libya, he had wanted us to be married without delay, so that I could go with him. I pointed out that since his prospecting work would keep him out in the desert for long periods of time, I'd be left alone in a strange city.

But actually my fear of loneliness was superseded by a reluctance to make the final commitment of marriage. He must have guessed that. At first, his letters described the attractive features of Tripoli, the friendly welcome he'd been given, the great variety of things from all over the world that could be found in the shops, and the pleasures of life in that warm, sunny climate. After the first few weeks he spoke only of his work, and then his letters became less frequent and oddly laconic.

The lights of a town appeared and disappeared. Then I saw the airport. The wheels touched down on the runway, the plane quickly slowed and stopped. Its engines fell silent.

My legs trembled slightly as I stood up, but my emotion didn't come from my first contact with Africa : I was about to see Philippe again and I was no longer sure I knew him very well.

I put on my coat, picked up my purse and left the plane. When all the other passengers had come out, a young woman wearing a dark uniform led us to the terminal building. In a dimly lighted room, long lines of people were waiting to have their papers checked. I didn't see Philippe anywhere.

The travelers were mostly Arabs, with a smattering of Italians and Americans. Their papers were all examined in minute detail. The wait seemed endless.

Suddenly I heard someone call out my name.

"Mademoiselle Montanier ? Geraldine Montanier ?"

A fat man ambled up to me. At first I thought Philippe, unable to come to the airport for some reason, had sent someone else to pick me up, but I was mistaken. The fat man represented the travel agency in charge of my accommodations and he knew nothing about Philippe Cottens. He spoke French with such a heavy Italian accent that I could have understood him better if he had spoken his own language, but I didn't want to offend him by telling him so.

He took my passport and the customs form I'd filled out, led me to the head of the line and gave voluble explanations in Arabic to the official there. Without saying a word in reply, the official stamped my papers and I went into the next room.

There again, no Philippe. The incoming passengers' baggage was lined up before two surly-looking customs officials who periodically picked out a suitcase at random and made its owner empty it completely. Still in Arabic, my guide interceded for me. My suitcases were marked with chalk and turned over to a porter wearing a red fez. A few minutes later I left the terminal.

The warm night was heavy with the fragrance of eucalyptus trees. A bus and several cars were parked in front of the door.

Till now I'd hoped Philippe would be waiting for me as I came out of the building. I had to face the fact that he simply wasn't there. He knew when my plane was scheduled to arrive; yet he hadn't come to meet me. For a moment I felt a rising panic, but I deliberately subdued it. There must have been some

misunderstanding, or perhaps Philippe was only
late.

The travel agency had sent a taxi for me, a black
and white Mercedes whose Arab driver spoke
Italian fluently. When my suitcases had been put
into the trunk, the fat man opened the rear door for
me. I refused to get in just yet. Philippe might arrive
at any minute and I wanted to wait.

Twenty minutes passed. The fat man had gone
back into the terminal; the bus and the cars had left.
I walked back and forth on the pavement, not
knowing what to do. When I became convinced that
I was waiting in vain, I resigned myself to going
alone to Tripoli.

I climbed into the taxi. During the trip, the driver
questioned me in a friendly way. Was this the first
time I'd ever been in Libya? Was I French? From
Paris? He had often had French passengers. He had
been told that Paris was a beautiful city.

His curiosity finally began to make me feel
uneasy. To turn the conversation away from myself,
I asked, "How far is Tripoli from the airport?"

"About twenty miles."

Since the airport was so far away, Philippe might
have come back to the city too late to make the trip.
He was probably waiting for me at the hotel.

We were driving through a dark countryside
where I could see the vague shapes of olive groves.
Finally white houses appeared, widely scattered at
first, then more numerous.

"Are we in Tripoli yet ?"

"Only on the outskirts. The city is spread out over a large area. That's the hospital over there. Nearly all the doctors are Italian. A few are Spanish."

"Are any French ?"

"Not that I know of. French doctors prefer to work in Tunisia."

We passed a stately residence surmounted by domes and encircled with gardens.

"That's the royal palace," said the driver. "And there's the Sidi Bellimam Mosque. The Hotel Uaddan is nearby. You'll be comfortable there. It's the best hotel in Tripoli."

I barely had time to see the minaret of the mosque when the taxi turned to the right and stopped. The driver pointed out the emblem above the entrance of the hotel: the head of a bearded antelope with long, curved horns.

"That's an uaddan. It's a desert animal that lives only in Libya."

A porter came to take my suitcases. When I tried to pay the driver he said, 'Everything is paid for by the agency. If you need me, call and ask for me at Transtourist. I'll always be ready to take you anywhere you want to go. My name is Musa ben Ahmed Karrun, but you can just ask for Musa."

He drove away and I entered the hotel.

The lobby was cluttered with the baggage of a group of Italians who had just arrived. I went to the reception desk and asked for Philippe's room number.

"Signor Cottens is no longer here," the clerk replied. "He checked out several days ago."

"That's impossible!" I exclaimed. "I called him here only two days ago!"

"Here? You must be mistaken. He wasn't here then."

Again I felt panic rising in me. I knew I'd called the Hotel Uaddan, though I couldn't have sworn I'd actually talked to Philippe. But I'd attributed the strange voice to a bad telephone connection. What if it hadn't been him at all? Who else could I have talked to? And why had he claimed to be Philippe?

Struggling to keep calm, I took the telegram from my purse and handed it to the desk clerk.

"Here, read this: he told me to meet him here."

The clerk read it, then turned it over and looked at the address.

"You're Geraldine Montanier?"

"Yes."

"The Transtourist Agency has reserved a room for you."

"I know, but what about—"

"I have a letter for you. Maybe it will answer your questions."

I eagerly seized the envelope he gave me. The address was typewritten but the letter, or rather the brief note, was in Philippe's handwriting:

I have to go away for a few days. I'll tell you why
when I come back, which will be as soon as
possible.

Philippe

Not a single affectionate word, not even a hint of
an explanation, yet the note reassured me. It really
was Philippe who had asked me to come to Tripoli; I
wasn't the victim of some sinister hoax, as I'd been
on the verge of believing. I examined the postmark.
The letter had been mailed the day before, in Tripoli.

"May I please have your passport?" asked the
desk clerk.

I gave it to him and filled out the registration
form. A porter was already waiting with my
suitcases, and I followed him to the elevator. Once I
was settled in the hotel, I'd have time to think over
Philippe's strange behavior.

My room was large, with white walls and a dark
blue ceiling. The furniture was commonplace, and
the window faced an equally commonplace building. I'd hoped for a view of the sea.

"That's the police headquarters," remarked the
porter.

As soon as he was gone, I sat down in an armchair
and critically examined my impersonal surround-
ings. Although very upset I didn't want to let myself
become completely disheartened. Since it was only
nine o'clock, I couldn't bear the thought of just
sitting there till I became sleepy enough to go to bed.

Without bothering to unpack, I went down the elevator and left the hotel.

Modern buildings flanked both sides of the street, and the Sidi Bellimam Mosque was brand-new. I walked to the nearby harbor, which, bordered by gardens and palm trees, was a beautiful sight. The lights of ships lying at anchor were reflected in the calm water. I followed the stone balustrade that ran along the shore. Probably because it was still dinnertime, I encountered very few other people and nothing interrupted my thoughts.

I was less worried since I'd read Philippe's note, but I was irritated by his lack of consideration. What was the sense of telling me to come to Tripoli as soon as I could if he wasn't even going to be there when I arrived? I'd never expected such thoughtlessness from a man who was regarded as a model of reliability by everyone who knew him.

The silence of the night and the soothing exercise of walking finally began to dissipate my ill humor. I decided that Philippe must have been forced to leave Tripoli by something beyond his control and was as sorry about it as I was. He wouldn't have changed his plans if he'd had any choice in the matter. Poor Philippe! I'd been judging him so harshly, yet in the past I'd always been so quick to forgive Eric's irresponsibility!

At least I'd been honest with him. When he asked me to marry him, six months after I'd broken off my secret engagement to Eric, I told him about the recent unhappy love affair, though I didn't mention the name of the man I'd loved. Philippe was acquainted with Eric. I knew he was unsure of himself and inclined to jealousy, so I wanted to avoid the tension that might arise if Eric happened to cross our path.

I had heard little about Eric since our breakup. I only knew that he was building roads in one of the former French colonies. It was a vague report and I hadn't tried to find out anything more specific. Eric was no longer part of my life.

After a time I became tired of the deserted waterfront and decided to look for a more animated part of the city. Turning into the first street that led away from the sea I soon came upon a broad, straight avenue. Stores lined both sides, but they were all closed, their iron curtains lowered.

Farther along the avenue was a large public square surrounded by majestic buildings. There was also an open gallery where the tables of a café were grouped around a fountain. The chairs were empty and the lights were all turned off. The scene gave the impression of a city in a state of siege. During my whole walk I'd passed no more than half a dozen people, each of whom regarded me suspiciously. The dismal, heavy atmosphere made me decide to return to the hotel.

BEFORE GOING UP to my room, I wandered through the galleries connecting the hotel with the gambling

casino in the same building. I stopped in front of a
stuffed uaddan standing against a background of
dark blue velvet. With his long, silky beard and
varnished hooves, he looked even more out of place
than I felt.

"Dina!"

Only one person in the world had ever called me
by that nickname, and I would have recognized his
voice anywhere. I turned around. In spite of his dark
suntan and a new bitterness in his eyes, he still had
the same arrogant, finely chiseled face and the same
nonchalant irony in his smile.

"Eric! What are you doing here?"

I realized that my presence must have startled
him as much as his had me, yet he betrayed very
little surprise. What had he been doing all those
months? I instinctively glanced at his left ring
finger. It was bare. He smiled and raised his hand.

"I'm still free. You, too?"

If he had been in Libya for any length of time, he
must have met Philippe, since Frenchmen weren't
numerous there.

"I'm not married yet, but you haven't answered
my question. What are you doing here?"

"In Libya? Making roads. In Tripoli? Presenting
some plans to the proper authorities. In the Hotel
Uaddan? I'm about to take you to dinner."

As if we'd left each other only the day before, he
took me by the arm and tried to lead me away. I held
back.

"Be serious, Eric. How long have you been, in Libya?"

"Six months."

"Then you must have seen Philippe. Do you know where he is?"

"I've met him two or three times, but he works mainly in the eastern part of the country and I work in the west, so we're usually hundreds of miles apart. Besides, I'm not terribly eager to see him. Why do you ask where he is? Have you lost him?"

He was gently making fun of me and was perfectly relaxed—too relaxed, as if he considered it only natural to see me there. A suspicion entered my mind.

"Did you know I was coming to Tripoli?" I asked.

"How could I have known? I'm not clairvoyant. Shall we continue this conversation in the hotel restaurant? I'm starving."

"No, thanks. I had dinner on the plane."

"Then come and keep me company while I eat."

"I don't feel like it."

"You seem to have a grudge against me. I can't imagine why."

"You really don't know?"

I thought I saw his face tense for a moment, but I couldn't be sure.

"I'm the one who ought to hold a grudge," he answered with a smile, "but let's not argue about it. Come with me."

I followed along, annoyed with myself for letting him control me as he'd done in the past.

He took me to a big restaurant that formed part of the casino. The tables surrounded a raised dance floor near bay windows veiled by thick curtains. An Italian orchestra was playing songs that dated from the time of my parents' adolescence. A swarm of waiters moved busily among the tables, serving the mostly male customers. A sprinkling of women in low-cut gowns graced the room, and I felt under-dressed in my traveling outfit.

"I should have changed.... Why are you laughing?"

. His laughter affected me deeply, like the nostalgic echo of a vanished dream.

"You're delightful, Dina. You've come all the way from Paris to find your fiancé, or so I gather. He's disappeared, and what concerns you most is the way you're dressed."

"Disappeared?" I asked anxiously. "Do you know something you haven't told me?"

"You asked me where he was, so I assume he's disappeared. That's all I know. I saw him a week ago and he seemed to be in the pink of health. Shall we order?"

A waiter stood beside our table.

"No, I couldn't—"

"Oh, come on, now! I'll order for you: a shrimp cocktail. Do you still like them as much as you used to?"

A feeling of unreality washed over me. Where was I? Eric kept his eyes on me, dark eyes in which I had seen reflected so many different emotions: love, joy, anger.

"What's brought you to Tripoli, Dina?" he asked when the waiter had left.

I told him what had happened: Philippe's telegram, my phone call, the note waiting for me at the hotel.

"Your parents let you leave?"

"I'm over twenty-one."

"But they didn't object? Lucky Philippe! He's in good standing with them, and if necessary you'd have defied them for his sake."

His tone was caustic. I could have understood his rancor if our breakup had been recent, but after all that time I was a little bewildered by his sarcasm.

"Don't make me regret dining with you. I was counting on your friendship."

"I've never felt any friendship toward you."

"Eric!"

I made a move to stand up, but he detained me with a hand on my arm.

"Stay, I'll behave myself. Tell me about your trip. When did you arrive?"

"Here at the hotel? About nine. I went out for a walk, but there wasn't much to see."

"You went out alone?"

"Yes."

"What do you know about Libya?"

I was irritated by the touch of superiority in his tone.

"You think I'm completely ignorant? You're forgetting that Philippe has been living here for eight months. He's told me a lot about the country in his letters."

Eric laughed unpleasantly.

"Philippe's letters! I can imagine what they're like!"

I wouldn't have expected him to feel brotherly love toward Philippe, but I was surprised by his scornful attitude.

"He writes very good letters," I said defensively.

"Did he happen to mention the subject of oil?"

"Of course, since he's—"

"Then maybe you know that Libya has become one of the largest oil-producing countries in the world. As a result, the Libyans have so much foreign currency they don't need tourists, which means that, unlike their neighbors the Tunisians, for example, they don't have to be friendly to foreigners. Keep that in mind and be careful. Don't go out at night without an escort."

Did he expect me to call on him for protection whenever I wanted to go somewhere? I bristled at the thought but kept my reaction to myself. We'd gone our separate ways and made new lives for ourselves, so what would be the sense of quarreling now?

"What have you been doing for the past two years, Eric? I heard you were working in Africa."

"That's right. I was in Niger and the Ivory Coast. When Libya decided to modernize its road system, I was sent here."

"So you're building roads?"

"Not yet. We're still doing preliminary studies. The plan is to build more than four thousand miles of new roads. That interests us. It also interests the Italians and the Americans. But the French aren't very fond of working in the desert."

"What about you? Doesn't the desert bore you?"

"It's easier to bear loneliness there."

I refrained from making any comment, but I doubted that he was as lonely as he implied, even though he wasn't married.

The dance floor was suddenly illuminated by spotlights and a woman in a green satin dress took hold of a microphone.

"You're about to discover the wild night life of Tripoli," Eric whispered.

The woman introduced a young sleight-of-hand artist, "for the first time in Libya." Wearing a black suit and cape, he began performing a series of tricks with varying degrees of success. Without once letting slip his smiling facade, he occasionally dropped an object or unintentionally revealed one hidden in his pocket. I watched his act abstractedly, more strongly affected by Eric's presence than I'd have thought possible. The old wound had healed, but there were too many memories between us.

I cast furtive glances at him. His long face and sharp features were the same, but there were little creases at the corners of his mouth that made him appear almost cruel.

I remembered what he had said about the desert. It was hard to imagine him lonely, and yet, in a way, he had been alone a long time. As an only child, orphaned young, he was placed in the care of a grandfather who had neither the time nor the patience to raise him. The old man had sent Eric off to boarding school as soon as possible.

But he was too independent to suffer insecurities from that kind of childhood. He had all the friends he could want, and I'd learned at my expense that he was very successful with women. How could my love have been enough for him? Yet I'd loved him as I would never love again, with all the blind, boundless devotion of youth. It had been a grim but useful lesson.

The magician finished his act and withdrew while his audience applauded indulgently. The orchestra launched into a waltz and couples began forming on the dance floor.

"Would you like to dance, Dina?"

"Not tonight."

He saw my hesitation and asked ironically, "Why not? Unsure of yourself?"

Without a word, I stood up and walked to the

dance floor. Did he think he still had the power to make me quiver with excitement? I had to make him realize that his conceit was misplaced. I was careful to show my indifference when he put his arm around me to begin dancing.

He had never been a good dancer. He was as tall as Philippe but less graceful, and I had to press my face against his shoulder to maintain a comfortable balance.

To make sure my action wouldn't be misinterpreted, I said laughingly, "I see you haven't made any progress."

He relaxed his hold and drew back to look at me.

"Philippe is a better dancer than I am?"

"Much better."

"Well, at least dancing is one way the two of you can have fun together!"

If he thought I was stung by that sarcastic remark, he was sadly mistaken. I had other things on my mind. Apparently Eric realized that, because as soon as we returned to our table he asked, "What are you going to do?"

"I'm not sure. For one thing, I suppose I'll get in touch with the people Philippe works with, and his friends."

"The people he works with are in Zelten, in the northeastern part of the country. As for his friends, I doubt he has any in Tripoli. Anyway, what could they tell you?"

"Where he is and why he left."

"How would they know? If he didn't tell you, he probably didn't tell anyone else. He must have reasons for keeping quiet on the subject."

"What are you trying to insinuate?"

He shrugged.

"Nothing. I'm only trying to think of an explanation, and that one's as good as any other."

"Is Philippe in some sort of trouble?"

"I'm not the one who could tell you that."

The unexpectedness of my meeting with Eric had made me forget my fears about Philippe. Anxiety suddenly came over me again, made worse by fatigue. Tears welled up in my eyes.

Eric pulled out his handkerchief.

"Here, dry your eyes and blow your nose. You'll feel better."

Exasperated, I pushed his hand away.

"Leave me alone! I've had a long, frustrating day and I'm tired. I'm going to my room now."

He stood up at the same time I did and, in spite of my protests, accompanied me to the elevator.

"Good night, Dina. If you need anything, call me. My room is on the fourth floor."

"Here? In this hotel?"

"Of course. The Uaddan is the best hotel in Tripoli, so my status requires me to stay here," he said with deliberate pomposity.

He had already begun walking away when he stopped, turned back and added, "If you want to question someone who knows Philippe, I've heard that he had some business dealings with an Italian lawyer whose name escapes me just now. I'll try to remember it and let you know."

I thanked him, glad at least that his feelings, whatever they were, hadn't meant he was completely unprepared to help me find Philippe.

As soon as I reached my room I threw off my clothes and climbed into bed. But sleep was impossible. Now and then the silence was broken by the sound of a car passing in the street below my window, or the furious yowling of stray cats. Lying in the darkness with my eyes wide open, I tried to straighten out my disordered thoughts.

Philippe ... was it possible he had something to hide? That idea should have made me smile. "He's a man you can count on," my father liked to say. *"He'll* never let you down," my mother would add. And their unspoken conclusion was, "He's not at all like Eric."

I'd never understood my parents' hostility toward Eric, even though events had proven them correct. It's true that we were both quite young when we met: I was eighteen and he was twenty-one. And, with his usual impetuosity, he'd spoken of marriage too soon. Yet it seemed to me that our impatience wasn't enough to justify a parental opposition that had held firm all through the years.

What did they have against him? He had graduated from high school with a brilliant record, then been accepted into engineering school after a

competitive examination that eliminated all but a
very small percentage of the candidates. But he
owed his success more to natural gifts than to hard
work. Were my parents suspicious of him because
things came too easily for him? Did they consider
him too handsome, charming and lighthearted to be
reliable? But whatever their reasons, they wouldn't
consent to my marrying him, and then, when we
became engaged in spite of their disapproval, they
demanded that we keep it a secret.

Maybe the main cause of their antagonism was
the intensity of my feelings for Eric. They doubted
that lasting happiness could be built on such
powerful, romantic passion.

I was sure I'd show them they were wrong. My
love resisted all their pressure and the delay they
imposed on our marriage. As soon as I was twenty-
one, I'd prove to them that my heart had been a good
judge. But then my illusions were suddenly
destroyed. . . .

Philippe, however, had pleased my parents from
the start. Older than Eric, he was already a man. He,
too, had graduated from a difficult course of studies,
but through hard, steady work. His perseverence
reassured them and they were glad I'd finally
stopped being deceived by appearances.

Even physically, Philippe reassured them. He was
tall, dark and more robust than Eric. Although his
mind worked more slowly, he succeeded in everything he undertook. And although he was awkward

when it came to declaring his love, I sensed his sincerity and total commitment to me.

As for Eric, no one had ever accused him of being a clumsy talker! I was often overwhelmed by the flow of his affectionate, admiring or passionate words. Even the nickname he invented for me had been a special way of expressing his love. And he still used it, even now....

Meeting him like that, as soon as I arrived in Tripoli, seemed strange, and although I couldn't have said why, it was also alarming.

Sleep was a long time in coming.

Chapter 3

Disoriented, I lay staring up at the dark ceiling for a few moments, before remembering: I was in Tripoli.

I stepped out of bed and opened the shutters. Against the intensely blue background of the sky, the white police building was flooded with sunlight; three palm trees swayed in the breeze; and a woman wearing a pink veil was walking across the courtyard. It was as hot as an August day in France.

The telephone rang.

"Dina? This is Eric. The Italian lawyer I told you about is named Arnelli, Attilio Arnelli. His office is on Bandona Street. You can call there and get the exact address."

"Thanks very much, Eric. I'll go see him."

"All right, but remember what I told you: be careful."

"Even in broad daylight?"

"Yes, even in broad daylight."

As soon as I'd hung up, I called the lawyer's office. He gave me a ten o'clock appointment.

I washed my face, combed my hair and put on a light summer dress. As I was about to leave, I remembered that I'd promised to send my parents a telegram when I arrived in Tripoli. They were probably beginning to worry now, but what could I tell them? The truth wouldn't do much to put their minds at rest. I composed a brief, noncommittal message—"Arrived safely letter to follow"—and gave it to the hotel switchboard operator, who promised that it would be sent immediately.

Before I wrote the promised letter, I'd have to see Philippe and learn the answers to the riddles running through my mind.

I left the hotel. Sunlight had transformed the city. Bright colors were everywhere: the dazzling white of the buildings, the blue of the sky and the sea, the orange yellow clusters of dates; bougainvillea displayed blazing hues in gardens; the red, stylized petals of poinsettias lined the sides of shady lanes, mingled with laurel bushes.

As I walked to Istiklal Avenue, the long street I'd followed the night before, I noticed that many of the iron curtains were still lowered. Traffic was heavy with trucks, taxis, private cars and even donkey carts. Sidewalks were crowded with young men wearing Western clothes and older men dressed in flowing burnouses. I spotted very few women.

I soon reached Bandona Street and easily found the dilapidated building where Arnelli's office was located. I was on time and he received me immediately.

A short man in his fifties, he had silver hair and a noble face, punctuated by shrewd, alert eyes sheltered by heavy eyelids. I spoke to him in Italian. He seemed surprised when I asked him if he knew where Philippe Cottens was.

"Signor Cottens came to consult me about a lease six or seven months ago, but I haven't seen him since."

"You've no idea where he might have gone?"

"No, I'm sorry. There's nothing I can tell you about him. I wish I could help you, but except for that matter of a lease, I wasn't his attorney. He dealt with one of my Libyan colleagues named Ahmed Salem. I'm going to see Salem at the courthouse in a few minutes. If you like, I'll tell him about your visit." He glanced at his watch. "I should be leaving now, as a matter of fact."

With an apologetic smile, he stood up to signal an end to our conversation.

"May I go with you?" I asked. "I'd like to meet Signor Salem."

He hesitated a second before answering, "Yes, of course. The courthouse is only a short walk from here."

On the way, he complimented me on my knowledge of Italian.

"I speak French very badly," he confessed with a smile. "If it weren't for your excellent Italian, I'm sure we wouldn't have been able to communicate at all."

"Italian seems to be a second language here. Are there many Italians in Tripoli?"

"About thirty thousand. We built the new part of the city. It's beautiful, isn't it? Ah, here we are."

Arnelli and I entered the courthouse and climbed a majestic staircase. On the second floor, he led me into an empty courtroom.

"Court will be in session shortly, but you can sit down and wait here. I'll come back as soon as I've met Salem."

He left the room and walked off down the hall. I sat on one of the benches reserved for the public. A few minutes later, men began coming in, nearly all of them in Arab dress. Then a few heavily veiled women arrived.

At first I was oblivious to the curiosity I aroused, but all those eyes staring at me finally made me realize I was the only unveiled woman in the room. I had the impression that my presence was considered shocking and before long I began feeling indecent because my face was bare.

When the court entered, I noticed that the magistrate and lawyers also gave me harsh looks. For the first time, I had the sensation of being an object of hostility, and it was all I could do to restrain myself from leaving.

Finally Arnelli appeared in the doorway and, to my immense relief, signaled me to join him in the hall.

"I've seen Salem," he told me. "He doesn't know where Signor Cottens is."

"I'd like to talk with him."

"He's already left."

Why had Arnelli waited till Salem was gone before returning to me? He knew I'd come to the courthouse for the specific purpose of meeting him.

"Where can I see him?"

"I suppose he'll be in his office, but he won't tell you anything more than what I've already said."

I had the distinct feeling that for some reason Arnelli didn't want me to see Ahmed Salem. Even so, he grudgingly gave me Salem's address and explained that it was near the Maidan Asoluhada. I said goodbye to him and left the courthouse.

ON MY WAY BACK to the hotel, I bought the Italian edition of a Tripoli newspaper and scanned it hastily in my room while I waited to go downstairs for lunch. I didn't know exactly what I hoped or feared to find. Its four pages contained only brief political news items, official announcements, advertisements and reports of crimes and accidents. There was nothing of particular interest to me.

In the restaurant, the curtains had been drawn back from the broad windows that overlooked the harbor. I chose a table, but before I had time to look over the menu, Eric strode over to me.

"Mind if I join you?"

Without waiting for an answer, he sat down, and his automatic assumption that I wanted his company irritated me.

"What if I do mind?"

"Be sensible, Dina. We're staying at the same hotel and I have to eat lunch, too. It would be ridiculous for me to sit at another table." He leaned toward me with a provocative smile. "Are you afraid of me?"

"I'm the last person in the world who'd be afraid of you. I know you too well."

He ignored my spiteful retort.

"Did you have a pleasant walk this morning?"

"I'm not here for pleasant walks. I came to meet Philippe, and until I've found him I won't concern myself with anything else."

"How do you plan to go about finding him? Are you going to use a crystal ball?"

I sighed and ignored his sarcasm.

"Or maybe you'd rather consult the police," he said, somewhat ambiguously. "They're in the building next door."

Was he trying to cast doubt on the legality of Philippe's activities?

"I'd notify the police if I thought he'd had an accident."

"If he had, it would have been reported in the local newspapers. They're very discreet in political

matters but they don't miss any accidents, crimes or
natural disasters—there aren't many other interesting things they can report. Look, Dina, you mustn't
let your imagination run away with you just
because you're in a foreign country. If Philippe had,
er, stood you up in France, you'd simply wait for
him to get in touch with you and explain his
reasons."

"I'm not in France."

"Have you begun your search?"

I told him about my visit to Arnelli and my futile
wait in the courthouse.

"Arnelli deliberately arranged things so that I
wouldn't meet Salem," I concluded. "I'm sure he's
hiding something from me."

"I'll bet you caused a sensation in the
courthouse!"

"You'd have thought I was sitting there in the
nude."

He laughed. "If you were in Kuwait you'd be
forced to wear a veil, even though you're French."

"You're kidding."

"Not at all. You've seen some Libyan women by
now. The way they're dressed, it's impossible to tell
them apart, but if you were to photograph one of
them without her husband's permission, your film
could be confiscated."

"I didn't bring a camera with me. Can't you get it
into your head that I'm not here as a tourist?"

"If you stay, you'll have a choice between sitting

in your room or going out and seeing the sights of the city, so you might as well be a tourist. Do you intend to marry Philippe?"

"What a question! We're engaged."

"What an answer! You and I were engaged, too."

"No, we weren't."

"Why do you say that? Because we didn't have your parents' blessing? I didn't know you were so traditional. Anyway, let's assume you marry Philippe. You'll have the rest of your life to be with him, but you'll be in Libya only a short time, so you should take advantage of your stay here. It's a country well worth seeing."

"With you as my guide?"

"No, I'm afraid not. Unfortunately I have to work. But I can go with you now and then. Starting the day after tomorrow, for example, I'll have two days off."

"I'd rather discover Tripoli with Philippe."

"Well, half a loaf is better than none. If you're willing to take second best, I'll be glad to offer you my humble company."

He laughed, but his eyes remained hard and he watched my face closely. What did he want? Whatever it was, I didn't want to know; everything had been said between us long ago.

I COULDN'T RESIGN myself to accepting Eric's two alternatives: either staying in my room or going out to see the sights of the city. There had to be some way of finding Philippe. What about the company he worked for? Should I call them in Zelten? I decided to do that only as a last resort, because I was afraid Philippe might have some reason for not wanting his employers to know he'd sent for me. He was so mysterious about it. . . .

My father had given me the name of a man he knew in the French embassy, just in case I needed some sort of help. I considered paying him a visit, but again I had misgivings. In his note, Philippe had told me that he was going away for a few days. He hadn't said where, and if he didn't want even me to know where he'd gone, he might very well not want anyone else to know either; so there was a good chance he wouldn't appreciate my reporting his absence to the embassy. And since he'd promised to explain when he returned, he might feel that my impatience betrayed a lack of trust.

A visit to Ahmed Salem was probably my best course of action. Philippe might still be annoyed, but at least I could count on Salem, his lawyer, to be discreet.

I called the Transtourist Agency and asked for Musa, the driver who had told me he would always be ready to take me anywhere I wanted to go.

Shortly afterward his black and white Mercedes pulled up in front of the hotel. Without knowing why, I felt it would be better not to let him know exactly where I was going. Arnelli had told me that Salem's office was near a public square called the Maidan Asoluhada, so that was where I asked Musa

to take me. He assumed I wanted to visit the old part
of the city, and I didn't say anything to make him
think otherwise.

When we arrived, he again refused to let me pay
him. The agency would take care of it, he said, and
before leaving he repeated that he would always be
at my disposal.

The Maidan Asoluhada straddled two worlds. On
one side, the wall of the ancient Arab city; on the
other, the broad, straight streets of the new city. I
waited till Musa's car was out of sight, then went to
Ahmed Salem's office on Omar Muctar Street.

I was told that he was out and would be back in an
hour. Not wanting to wait in his office, I decided to
stroll through the Arab quarter.

Tripoli had changed little in the four centuries
since the seige of the Spanish who granted the city to
the Knights of St. John. Its line of fortifications still
stood, and its streets formed an intricate maze, like
those in all Casbahs.

I stopped to watch a group of craftsmen hammer-
ing copper and carving olivewood. The simplicity of
a nearby mosque was beautiful. Facing the wall, two
men were praying while a third washed himself in
the water of a fountain. Farther on, vendors loudly
hawked their wares in an open-air market.

I began strolling through little streets that wound
their way among low houses. In some places the
roads were so narrow that hardly any sunlight
penetrated them. But they were full of life: bright-

eyed children playing tirelessly, men talking in groups or strolling, women wearing pink or white veils.

Wandering at random, I crossed the entire section without seeing another European; yet I had no feeling of insecurity at any time. Many people looked at me with curiosity or indifference, but never with animosity.

On the other side of the ramparts stood the triumphal arch built by Marcus Aurelius when Tripoli was a Roman colony. A new mosque, painted bright green, rose above the arch. Beyond it lay the sea.

I was gazing at the mosque when I noticed a young man in his early twenties, wearing navy blue trousers and a gray shirt. He looked vaguely familiar, but I couldn't remember where I had seen him.

I glanced at my watch and realized it was time to go back to Ahmed Salem's office on Omar Muctar Street. I began to thread my way back through the maze of the old city, but soon, much to my dismay, became lost. Coming to a dead end, I retraced my steps and followed a quiet street, empty but for a lone woman in front of me. Then I heard footsteps behind me. I looked around and saw the young man in the gray shirt. Suddenly I remembered where I'd seen him before: in the courthouse, that morning. Was it only a coincidence? Instinctively quickening my pace, I wished I could be sure.

I turned right and came to an intersection. Squatting on his heels, an old man was sifting grain. His expressionless gaze lingered on me a moment, then moved on. I glanced over my shoulder. The young Arab was still there. By now I was convinced he was following me.

I recalled Eric's warning and wished I'd taken it more seriously. Did that man intend to rob me? If he snatched my purse, no one would intervene. I wasn't carrying much money, but I would hate to lose all my papers.

I was gripped by unreasoning fear. My only thought was to reach the modern city as quickly as possible, but I was lost and felt I'd been going in circles. The man still followed close behind me, but I was afraid to stop and ask someone for directions. My self-control crumbled and I began running wildly, straight ahead, oblivious to everything but my fear.

I stumbled on the uneven cobblestones and fell to my knees, dropping my purse. Its contents spilled out.

"Did you hurt yourself, mademoiselle?"

My follower had questioned me in impeccable French. He crouched and began picking up the scattered objects from my purse.

"No, I'm all right."

"Why were you running?" he asked reproachfully.

I gave him the first explanation that entered my

mind: "I'm late for an appointment and I've lost my way."

He handed back my purse and helped me to my feet.

"Where is your appointment?"

"On the Maidan Asoluhada."

"That's not far away. Would you like me to guide you?"

"No ... no, thanks. Just tell me how to get there."

To my great relief, he gave directions without insisting on accompanying me, and I easily reached the Maidan Asoluhada. Now that I felt safe again, I couldn't understand the panic that had come over me. Why had I attributed evil intentions to that young man? He'd happened to be going in the same direction I was, that was all. My frantic running now seemed ridiculous. I blamed Eric: his warning had made me skittish.

AHMED SALEM, a man of about forty with a pockmarked face, welcomed me cordially into his office. We spoke in Italian.

"I was told you came to see me while I was out," he said. "I'm sorry you had to wait, especially as there's nothing I can tell you about Signor Cottens."

"But he's your client, isn't he?"

"I handled a legal matter for him about six months ago. I haven't heard from him since."

I remembered that Arnelli had mentioned a lease.

"Did he consult you about renting something?" I asked.

"Yes, an apartment. There was a dispute over it but it was settled and the lease was signed."

Philippe had said nothing about an apartment in any of his letters.

"Does he still have it?"

"I don't know. As I told you, that was six months ago. He may have moved out of it by now."

"Can you give me the address?"

Silence. Was he hesitating for the same reason Arnelli had when I asked if I could accompany him to the courthouse? He shrugged fatalistically.

"Number seven, Balatra Street, on the seventh floor."

With a sense of excitement I left his office. At last I had some precise information. I was intrigued by the apartment that Philippe hadn't seen fit to tell me about.

I reached Balatra Street after a ten-minute walk. Number seven was a fairly modern building. In the entrance hall, rows of small mailboxes, each with a name on it, were arranged according to floors. No Philippe Cottens was listed. Apparently he no longer lived there, as Salem suggested. Even so, I took the elevator to the seventh floor.

There were three doors on the landing, with the tenants' names on them. None displayed Philippe's. But if he'd once lived there, maybe one of the other

tenants had known him and could tell me something about him.

I rang two doorbells without receiving an answer.
The third door was opened by a slender young
woman with tousled blond hair. She looked at me
suspiciously.

"Do you know Philippe Cottens?" I asked in
Italian.

My question had a remarkable effect: she turned
pale and her lips began quivering.

"Who? I didn't catch the name."

She spoke Italian with such a heavy French
accent that I answered her in French, since that was
obviously her native language.

"I'm looking for Philippe Cottens."

"I don't know anyone by that name."

She slammed the door in my face. I stood on the
landing, disheartened. Had the trail I thought I'd
discovered been cut off?

THE SUN WAS SETTING as I walked back to the hotel.
For all I'd accomplished, I might just as well have
spent the day in my room. I felt dejected and
resentful. Why hadn't Philippe told me to delay my
departure till he returned to Tripoli, instead of
making me wait in a foreign city, wondering where
he could be and why he had left?

My resentment was mingled with uneasiness.
Salem and Arnelli had answered my questions; yet

I'd sensed unmistakable reticence in both of them. Even Eric. . . .

Near the Hotel Uaddan, on the ground floor of a corner building, was a large store. As I crossed the street, I glanced at its display window and saw the reflection of a man behind me. He wore a gray shirt and navy blue trousers. I was sure it was the same young man I'd encountered in the old city, but cars were passing and I had to wait till I reached the other side of the street before I could turn around. By then he was nowhere in sight. Had I been mistaken? After all, how could I make a positive identification from a reflection in a window?

In the hotel, I approached the reception desk to ask if anyone had left a message for me. Nothing. I couldn't shake off the feeling that Philippe had forgotten me.

Wanting to avoid Eric, I came down early for dinner but found he was already waiting for me. And refusing to sit at his table might have given our meeting an importance that it didn't have.

He asked me how I'd spent the afternoon. I described my visit to Ahmed Salem, but not the fright I'd had in the old city.

"Did you know Philippe had rented an apartment?" I asked.

"No, but what's so unusual about renting an apartment?"

"It seems strange to me that he did so in Tripoli,

when he works hundreds of miles away. It also seems odd that he never mentioned it to me."

"He comes to Tripoli now and then. Perhaps he just decided he'd rather stay in an apartment than a hotel."

"Well, he doesn't have it any more. I went there to see if I could find out anything."

"You went to Balatra Street?"

I stared at him in surprise.

"You know the address?"

"You told it to me just now."

I was certain I hadn't, but we were no longer on close enough terms for me to call him a liar.

"What are you trying to find out, Dina?" he went on. "Remember what happened to Bluebeard's wife because of her curiosity."

"Thanks for the comparison. But you don't really think I'm in danger, do you?"

"It depends on what you mean by danger."

"I'm getting tired of your vague hints, Eric! If you know something, say it!"

"I just wanted to remind you that if you pry into people's lives, you may make some unpleasant discoveries."

"I'm not prying into Philippe's life. Even if I did, I'm sure I wouldn't discover anything unpleasant. And he is, after all, my fiancé."

"Suit yourself," he said flippantly. Then his face became serious. "Take my advice and be patient. Wait until you hear from Philippe and don't try to track him down. That's the best thing you can do, believe me."

"Why?"

He changed the subject without answering.

When we finished dinner, I said I was tired and wanted to go up to my room. But Eric had other plans for me.

"Let's go for a walk. I want to talk with you."

"You've already been talking with me. And besides, you told me I shouldn't go out at night."

"You'll be safe with me. We won't go far from the hotel."

If he had something to tell me, why hadn't he done it during dinner? But, with the hope that he might have decided to tell me what he knew about Philippe, I agreed.

The night was warm. The minaret of the Uaddan shone like a reassuring lighthouse. We walked to the waterfront, exchanging only a few insignificant words. Eric leaned his elbows against the balustrade. I waited for him to speak but he remained silent.

Finally I asked, "Do you know where he is?"

"Who?"

"Philippe, of course!"

"Never mind Philippe! We're not here to talk about him; we're here to talk about us!"

"Us?"

"Yes, us, and especially our breakup. You wouldn't listen to me and you even sent back my letters unopened. I think I have a right to an explanation."

It was too dark for me to see his face, but he sounded as if he were talking about something that had happened only the day before.

"Why dig up the past, Eric? I don't hold anything against you."

"That's no surprise, since I'm not the one who refused to listen."

Wanting to avoid a quarrel, I said in a conciliatory tone, "All right, let's say I was in the wrong. But it's too late to go back now."

"I don't see why, since you've already shown that you don't mind breaking an engagement."

"What was there to break? You never really committed yourself to me."

"That's not true. But don't worry, I'm not trying to bring us back together. I just want to be judged fairly. You owe me a chance to explain the incident that you used as an excuse for breaking your word to me."

"You think *I* broke *my* word to you?"

"You promised to marry me as soon as you were twenty-one, and then two months before—"

"I discovered you were unfaithful."

"Unfaithful? Because I took a cousin's friend out for dinner a few times? She was alone and lost. She meant nothing to me and had no effect on my love for you. I'm not claiming it was perfectly all right for me to do what I did without explaining the circumstances, but it really wasn't very serious. If you'd loved me. ..."

In spite of my efforts to remain detached, I felt anger rising in me. Why was Eric reopening old wounds? He was incapable of being faithful and I was incapable of accepting unfaithfulness. It was as simple as that.

"I didn't expect you to close your eyes," he said slowly, "but I did hope you'd forgive me, because of ... extenuating circumstances. I was young, separated from you, and alone in a foreign country."

"Alone? Not quite. You had a few women to keep you company—one at a time, I suppose, though I can't be sure."

"I took out women for company, but none of them mattered to me."

"At least one of them did, since your 'little dinners' with her lasted several months."

"No, they didn't! You were misinformed."

"Let's not quibble over details, Eric. The fact is that you and I have very different ideas about love. You'd have liked me to be part of your harem, but I wanted a husband who would love only me."

"You're mistaken. I've loved only once in my life. I'd have been a faithful husband. But you ruined everything with your stubbornness and your stupid engagement to Philippe."

My anger flared up again. His rancor was the result of wounded vanity: maybe he felt a certain sadness at having lost me, but mainly he was offended because I'd replaced him with someone else.

"My engagement isn't stupid, and I refuse to listen to any more of your—"

"Be honest with me, Dina. Do you really love Philippe, the way you and I loved each other?"

"No two situations are ever the same. I'm too old to be satisfied with dreams now. You and I dreamed together; I've chosen to live instead. The future Philippe and I will have together won't be built on sand."

I heard him laugh in the darkness.

"On sand, you can only put up a tent, but a tent that belongs to you is better than a rented apartment or a hotel room. Are you sure you have no regrets, Dina?"

"No more than you do."

He laughed again.

"I've stopped having any."

Chapter 4

When I was back in my hotel room, I wondered why Eric had brought up the subject of our separation. One reason had probably been a desire to justify himself, but when I thought back over our conversation it seemed to me that he must also have wanted to let me know that he'd replaced me. He said he no longer had any regrets. Why? No doubt because he'd found someone else. So he hadn't been referring to me when he said he'd loved only once in his life.

His accusations still irritated me. It was incredible that he blamed me for our breakup! He didn't deny that he'd been unfaithful; yet he claimed I was in the wrong because I wouldn't forgive him!

When Philippe asked me to come to Tripoli, had he realized he'd be giving me a chance to see the man I'd loved in the past? At least I could now tell him there was no longer any reason for him to be jealous. Eric had found a new love and stopped caring about me. I should have been glad to know that, but instead I felt resentment I had no right to feel, and sadness I couldn't explain.

AT TEN O'CLOCK the next morning I was awakened by the jangling of the telephone. It was Signor Arnelli calling to invite me to dinner at his home that evening. His wife, he said, was looking forward to meeting me. Although the invitation was completely unexpected I accepted it. Arnelli obviously hadn't told me everything he knew; I hoped he'd changed his mind and decided to be more open when he saw me again.

I called the reception desk to ask if there were any letters or messages for me and was again disappointed. I began wondering how much longer I'd have to stay in Tripoli. I hadn't brought much money. I didn't know how much my room cost but, judging from the prices in the restaurant, I was afraid I wouldn't be able to pay the bill if I stayed very long.

I called the desk again to ask the price of my room. The clerk told me that all my expenses were being taken care of by the Transtourist Agency. That reassured me; Philippe had made arrangements for everything. I should have expected it, knowing how methodical he was. Then the clerk added that although my room had been reserved for only three weeks, I could stay longer if I wished. This information came as such a shock that I hung up without saying a word in reply.

Three weeks! Philippe had asked me to come as quickly as possible; yet he had left Tripoli after making a three-week reservation for me! What could that mean? I was completely bewildered. I decided not to tell anyone about my discovery, especially not Eric.

At lunch, Eric made no reference to our conversation of the previous night. Instead, he began telling me about the road-building projects he was engaged in.

"How long will you stay in Libya?" I asked.

"Several months. When the preliminary studies are finished, I'll return to France."

"And then you'll get married?"

My question caught him off guard. But he quickly recovered and answered with a smile, "If it were up to me." Then he abruptly changed the subject.

When we left each other, I derived a certain pleasure from telling him that I wouldn't see him at dinner that evening. He asked me to spend the next day with him. I refused at first, then gave in. Now that I knew he was in love with someone else, there was no need for me to be afraid that he might try to revive the past.

In the afternoon I visited a museum that occupied an old castle overlooking the sea. There was little else I could think of to do, and I felt that a change of scene might help me to clarify my thoughts.

After looking at a collection of mosaics, I climbed
to the top of the castle. A panorama of the whole city
was spread before me: the minarets and white
domes, the long avenues still under construction in
the outlying districts, the harbor, with ships at
anchor and fishing boats tied alongside docks, the
glittering blue sea beyond.

I leaned against the parapet and unanswered
questions began running through my mind. What
would I do if a long time went by without any word
from Philippe? I couldn't accept the idea of
returning to Paris without having seen him. Would
Arnelli give me some valuable explanations that
evening? And what about Eric? I was sure he knew
more than he'd told me.

I couldn't help wondering about the woman he'd
fallen in love with. What was she like? Did he love
her enough to be faithful? He hadn't been faithful to
me and had admitted it in so many words. I was hurt
by that admission; it tarnished the past and spoiled
the memory of my first love. Until my conversation
with him the night before, I was convinced that
neither of us would ever experience anything as
intense as the love we'd shared, but now I knew he'd
found something else with another woman.

I drove such bitter thoughts from my mind and
went down to the section of the museum containing
stuffed specimens of Sahara animals: jackals,
hyenas, foxes, porcupines, gazelles and uaddans. The
guard told me that uaddans were a vanishing

species; the last survivors could be found only in remote regions of the Libyan Desert. Jackals were numerous, however, and still threatened livestock in areas near Tripoli.

As I was leaving the museum I spotted the young Arab who had followed me the day before. He was slowly walking in my direction on the other side of the street. I'd forgotten about him. I tried to convince myself that my repeated encounters with him were only chance, and without looking at him again, I followed the ramparts to Adrian Pelt Street. When I reached the two high pillars on either side of the stairs that led down to the sea, I glanced over my shoulder. He was behind me.

There was no longer any doubt that he was deliberately following me. I felt I ought to walk up to him and ask him what he wanted, but I didn't have the courage. Besides, it would have been easy for him to pretend innocence.

He was beginning to worry me. Had someone hired him to keep an eye on me? And if so, who? And for what reason? I couldn't imagine why anyone should be seriously interested in knowing how I spent all my time away from the hotel. I decided that the young man must be acting on his own: he'd seen me walking around the city on my own, found me attractive and was following me in the hope of perhaps getting to know me. It was a plausible explanation, and if true, might cause me some annoyance, but at least wouldn't be a threat to my safety. Even so, I intended to be on my guard.

ARNELLI HAD INSISTED on picking me up at the hotel. He arrived at eight o'clock sharp.

"It's better not to go out alone at night," he said as we drove off in his car.

"The streets aren't safe?"

"Maybe yes, maybe no. But it's always a good idea to be careful."

His apartment was on the top floor of a luxurious building in the center of the city. His wife made a point of letting me know that they also owned a house in the country where they spent vacations and occasional weekends.

She was a short, plump woman who had probably once been attractive but had now given up the struggle to keep her figure slim. The sumptuous dinner she had prepared was rich in calories, and she consumed huge portions with obvious relish. At the same time she somehow managed to keep up a steady stream of talk that reduced her husband to silence.

When we finished our meal and entered the living room for coffee, she asked me if I'd heard from my fiancé.

During my conversation with Arnelli in his office, I hadn't told him the exact circumstances of my visit to Tripoli. Although still resisting the idea that Philippe might have something to hide, I couldn't ignore the fact of his unusual behavior, and I preferred to give an altered version of the facts.

I told Signora Arnelli that I'd unexpectedly been given time off from my job in Paris and decided on the spur of the moment to come and see Philippe in Tripoli, without letting him know in advance; unfortunately he was gone when I arrived, and I was eager to find him before my short vacation ended.

She sympathized with me, and once again I asked Arnelli if he could give me any suggestions as to how I might go about finding Philippe. He repeated that there was nothing useful he could tell me.

"How long has your fiancé been in Libya?" asked his wife.

"Eight months."

"You never wanted to come to visit him before now?"

"Libya is a long way from Paris; besides, he doesn't have much time off from his work."

"Did he tell you not to come?"

"No, of course not. It's just that I never had an opportunity till now."

"But you didn't tell him you were coming. Were you afraid he'd be against it?"

"I'm sure he'll be delighted to see me."

"Does he write to you often?"

"Yes."

"Does he tell you about his work and his friends?"

Her indiscreet questions were beginning to exasperate me, and I had to make an effort to restrain myself from telling her so.

Arnelli sensed my feelings.

"Please excuse my wife's curiosity," he said. "She's taken a liking to you, and that's why she wants to understand."

"Understand what?"

"Why you came here without being sure you'd see your fiancé."

"He'd written me that he was in Tripoli."

They dropped the subject and began suggesting things I could do during my stay in Libya. Arnelli told me that I ought to see the ancient Roman ruins at Sabrata and Leptis Magna. He and his wife would be glad to take me there, he said.

"Thank you for offering," I replied, "but I think Philippe may want to take me to those places, and he'd be disappointed if I'd already seen them. In the meantime there's plenty of sightseeing for me to do in Tripoli, though I must admit I'm looking forward to making an excursion into the desert. I'd love to see some camels, for example."

"Camels? They're not hard to find. Didn't you see any on the way from the airport?"

"It was dark when my plane landed."

"Go to the Giumia market tomorrow morning and you'll see all the camels you want."

"Your fiancé must have told you about that

market," said Signora Arnelli. "Do you intend to come back to Libya after you're married?"

And she launched into another interrogation. Arnelli appeared somewhat embarrassed by her indiscretion, but I noticed he listened attentively to my answers.

I'd come there in the hope of finding out some useful information. I now had the strong feeling that they'd invited me to dinner for the specific purpose of questioning me. Was it only idle curiosity, or was my presence in Tripoli cause for concern?

THE NEXT MORNING I awoke early and made my usual call to inquire if there was any word from Philippe. The desk clerk sounded as if he regretted having to disappoint me again.

Except for the cryptic note that had been waiting for me when I first arrived at the hotel, Philippe had left me completely in the dark. It wasn't like him to be so inconsiderate, and I didn't know whether to be worried or angry. Anger finally won out, because it seemed unlikely that anything could have happened to him without my being notified. As a kind of revenge, I decided to pass the time as pleasantly as I could without him.

I'd agreed to spend the day with Eric but I wasn't supposed to meet him till ten-thirty. That would give me time to visit the market that the Arnellis had told me about. I called the Transtourist Agency and asked if Musa could drive me there.

When I went down to the foyer half an hour later, after a quick breakfast in my room, Musa was waiting for me.

The Giumia market was in a village three miles outside the city. On the way, Musa told me he had three children and proudly showed me pictures of them. He didn't mention his wife and I didn't broach the subject because I'd been told it was very bad form to ask a Moslem about his wife.

The road, shaded by eucalyptus trees, was heavily traveled by cars, carts and people on foot. When we entered a village with low white houses, Musa pulled off the road and stopped.

"This is where the market is," he announced. "I'll wait for you here."

Following the crowd, I found myself in a courtyard where grain was being sold. Merchants squatted beside bulging sacks, into which they plunged rough hands, letting the grain trickle between their fingers. Donkeys laden with enormous baskets were being led through the dense mob of people. The brilliant sunlight missed nothing, transforming wheat or oats into tiny gold nuggets, restoring whiteness to threadbare wool garments and adding luster to the green fronds of palm trees.

I moved on to another courtyard where fruit and vegetables were on display. Finally I happened across the animal market. Inside a large pen enclosed by whitewashed walls were sheep, goats, cows, donkeys and camels.

Arnelli had been right: there were camels—all dromedaries, the single-humped variety—of every size, age and color, from dirty white to dark brown, with a wide range of tans in between. Some were hobbled, others had one leg tied to a stake. A few were muzzled. Indifferent to the bustle and noise of the market, they stood swaying tirelessly on their fragile-looking legs, chewing imaginary grass with their yellow teeth.

"Do you speak Italian, signorina?"

A tall man of about fifty, wearing a fez, had come up to me.

"I'm French, but I understand Italian," I answered.

"I've never been to France, but once I was in Rome."

With an affability I found reassuring, he told me that he and his camels had appeared in several Italian films. We chatted for a few minutes about camels, a subject he obviously knew well, then he politely excused himself and walked away. I'd enjoyed our brief conversation and I was sure that, other than just a desire to be friendly, he'd had no ulterior motive for approaching me.

Suddenly a deafening roar made me look up. A group of jets from a nearby military airfield were streaking across the clear sky. I watched them till they disappeared behind a palm grove. When I lowered my gaze I found the young Arab in the gray shirt directly in my line of vision.

How had he known I was going to the market, when I'd decided only at the last minute? I had an impulse to run, but the crowd was so thick that my progress through it was agonizingly slow. I edged toward the right and found myself near the camels—too near. I stepped back, bumped into a donkey, narrowly missed being kicked by a calf and stumbled into the midst of a flock of foul-smelling sheep.

Totally unperturbed, the young man continued to follow me. I headed back toward the camels. He did the same. I began to lose my head. Although I tried to convince myself that nothing could happen to me there, surrounded by so many people, I felt that my safety depended on quickly getting back to Musa and his Mercedes.

I frantically pushed my way through the crowd, roughly shoving people aside with my hands and elbows. I heard angry exclamations, but by then I was in such a panic that I didn't care what anyone thought of my behavior.

At last I reached the road. When I saw the black and white car I broke into a run. Musa got out and anxiously came forward to meet me.

"What's the matter, signorina?"

I looked back. My follower had fallen farther behind me, but he was still there, on the road.

"Musa, do you know that man?"

"I don't think so. Has he been bothering you?"

I restrained an insane impulse to laugh. Although

I couldn't accuse him of doing anything wrong, to say that he'd bothered me would have been a monumental understatement.

"No," I answered. "It's only that . . . I thought I'd seen him before. It doesn't matter. Please just take me back now."

Chapter 5

It was nearly eleven when Musa dropped me off in front of the hotel. Eric was pacing back and forth on the sidewalk, waiting for me. From a distance he reminded me of Philippe, because they were both tall and dark, but there the resemblance ended.

"You have an odd look on your face," he said to me. "Where have you been?"

"I'm sorry I'm late. I went to the Giumia market."

"Was it interesting?"

I nearly told him about the man in the gray shirt, but changed my mind. Eric would have made fun of me.

"The most interesting part of it was the camels— the dromedaries."

"You don't have to be so specific," he said with a smile. "You can just call them camels like everyone else."

"Well, whatever, I enjoyed seeing them."

"It was foolish of you to wander around the place alone."

"I wasn't exactly alone. It was so crowded I could hardly move."

"That's not the point. . . ."

"The point is that nothing happened to me."

Eric dismissed my argument with a shrug and took me by the arm. He led me to a Fiat parked beside the curb and opened the passenger door.

"We can indulge ourselves," he said. "It's a company car."

The upholstery wasn't in very good condition but the engine ran smoothly. Eric drove with the easy self-assurance that I remembered from the past.

"Where are we going?" I asked.

"First we'll have lunch at a seaside restaurant outside the city."

"And then?"

"I'll take you for a drive and show you some of the countryside around Tripoli. We can go to Sabrata and see the Roman ruins there. How does that suit you?"

"It suits me very well."

I answered without hesitation, even though I'd meant it when I told Arnelli the night before that I didn't want to make any sightseeing excursions till Philippe came back. I felt differently now. Why should I worry about disappointing Philippe when he was treating me so inconsiderately?

We drove out of the city and through the suburbs. Finally Eric turned off the main road and stopped the car at the edge of a long beach with sea gulls wheeling above it.

The restaurant was a short walk away. It was crowded but Eric had reserved a table for us, beside a window. The menu offered a choice of Arabic and Italian food. Preferring to stay on familiar ground, I ordered only Italian dishes.

"You're not tempted by the local cuisine?" Eric asked when the waiter had left our table. "Wouldn't you like to try a camel steak?"

"Have you ever eaten camel?"

"More often than you might think. In small towns and villages it's very common."

"Is it good?"

"Yes, if it comes from a young animal. I don't like the meat of old ones, but apparently everyone doesn't agree with me, because a lot of them are eaten. Most of the camels you saw in the market this morning will be sold to butchers."

"I wish you hadn't told me that. I'd imagined their being ridden back into the desert where they came from."

"They come mainly from Tunisia."

"So much for romantic fancy."

The heat and the sunlight glittering on the sea gave me a feeling of being on a summer vacation, and I even forgot for the time being why I was in Libya. Eric was looking at me intently. In his dark eyes I saw the glow I'd once attributed to love. How mistaken I'd been!

"Why haven't you told me anything about that woman?" I asked.

He looked puzzled.

"What woman?"

"The one who's driven away your regrets."

For a moment he seemed not to understand, then he laughed.

"You're jealous?"

"Don't be absurd! But we've known each other too long to keep secrets from one another. You know everything about me; you know how much I love Philippe. . . ."

"No, I don't know that and I don't want to. Never mind Philippe; I've already heard more than enough about him. Do you remember Mortefontaine?"

The blood rushed to my cheeks. Yet there was nothing shameful about the memories that name awakened. Eric and I had known each other only a short time when we went with a group of friends to spend a day in the country near Mortefontaine. While we were talking lightheartedly with the others, our eyes had met. Not a word, not a gesture, but at that moment we both became aware of our mutual attraction.

So vivid was my memory of the magic of that revelation that I couldn't remain impassive when I heard Eric refer to it. My surge of emotion didn't escape him and I knew him well enough to realize that it pleased him.

He began mentioning other names, recalling other images, reforging link by link the chain of days that had united us. I wanted to tell him to stop, but refusing to listen to his reminiscences would have been an admission that they still had the power to wound me.

Then I, too, began bringing up memories, but in an amused tone, lingering over the comical aspects. I laughed indulgently, as if looking at yellowed photographs in a family album. Eric echoed my laughter. And thus we cheerfully disowned our most precious moments together.

His responses, however, gradually became fewer and fewer, until finally I was talking by myself. When he bowed his head, I stopped. He had begun that cruel game, but he was the first to grow weary of it.

"You're right," I said. "It's not funny."

He looked up at me. There were tears in his eyes.

"Eric, what's the matter?"

"Nothing. Just the glare of the sunlight in my eyes."

It wasn't a convincing explanation. Seized with remorse, I realized I'd been on the defensive ever since our first meeting in Tripoli. I'd thought only of myself, without wondering if his eagerness to see me was caused by a need to escape from loneliness. Because he was in love, I'd assumed he was happy, but maybe he had reasons to be sad in spite of his love.

"Eric, I don't want to be indiscreet, but if I can help you...."

I put my hand on his and felt him start.

"Help me, Dina?" he asked softly.

He leaned down and kissed my wrist. The touch of his lips affected me so strongly that I sat motionless, staring at his bowed head, until he murmured, "Don't worry, Dina, I'm happy."

BUT HE DIDN'T SEEM at all happy when we got back into the car and headed for Sabrata.

We drove through the countryside, where low earthen walls marked off enclosures containing fig trees, agaves and giant cacti. Here and there were wells with wooden beams bracing them; from a distance they resembled the horns of an enormous gazelle. Barefoot children played in the red dust around cubical houses. Donkeys and camels grazed peacefully beneath palm trees.

I noticed that most of the other cars we passed on the road were driven by Libyans. Members of the large Italian colony in Tripoli apparently didn't venture out into the country very often.

"Do you have many Libyan friends?" I asked.

"I have quite a few, especially among the people I work with."

"And how about Philippe? Does he also have Libyan friends?"

Eric pointed beyond an olive grove to white
pillars rising in the distance.

"Look, there's Sabrata."

"You haven't answered my question."

He shrugged impatiently.

"How many times do I have to tell you that I don't
want to talk about Philippe?"

"But you used to be friends, didn't you?"

"We still are, officially. But your engagement
hasn't exactly brought us closer together."

"I've never told him that you and I were once
engaged."

"That doesn't surprise me."

"Then why should he have anything against
you?"

Eric turned to look at me.

"Hasn't it ever occurred to you that I might not
enjoy the company of the man who's replaced me?"

"That's ridiculous! I'd be glad to know the
woman you love!"

He didn't answer. From his expression I could see
that it would be useless for me to insist.

The ruins of Sabrata were spread out along the
shore, dominated by the imposing mass of the
amphitheater. Throughout the centuries, the isola-
tion of the ancient city had protected it from being
pillaged by builders in search of stone and its
outlines remained intact. The dividing walls were
still standing, the streets still had their paving

stones, and statues still watched over crumbling temples.

I listened to Eric's comments distractedly, trying to understand.

When we came to the amphitheater, we climbed to the top tier of seats. There, with the wind from the sea clutching at our clothes, we had a breathtaking view of the ruins. On our way back down, my foot slipped on the smooth stone and Eric caught me. When I felt his arms around me, an inexplicable weakness assailed me, and long seconds passed before I freed myself from his grip. I looked quickly at him and was surprised by his expression: he appeared on the verge of laughing. I continued gingerly down the steps, puzzled by his amusement and the shakiness I still felt in my legs.

On the drive back to Tripoli, while the shadows of the palm trees were lengthening and the sky was turning a brilliant pink, Eric seemed to be in a carefree mood. I thought he was trying to make me forget his tears, the first ones I'd ever seen him shed.

But when we entered the city he became more serious.

"What are your plans for tomorrow?" he asked.

"I haven't decided yet."

"You're still determined to keep on trying to find Philippe?"

"Of course."

"I can't stop you, but I hope you'll at least be more careful than you were this morning."

"What do you mean?"

"I've already told you it was foolish of you to wander around the Giumia market alone."

"And I've already told you that I was safe in the middle of that crowd. Besides, my driver would have protected me if necessary."

"I don't see how, since he parked his car beside the road and stayed there."

"How do you know that?" I asked sharply.

"I just assumed it. I've been to that market, too. I know that cars are parked along the road, and I've seen drivers waiting in them."

It was plausible. I rejected the suspicion that had sprung up in my mind. Eric couldn't have been watching me at the market without my noticing him, and it was ridiculous to suspect him of having gone there to spy on me.

We stopped at a restaurant for dinner, then drove to the hotel. He came into the lobby with me, but said he wanted to take a walk before going to his room. I was a little surprised that he didn't ask me to go with him, though I probably would have refused, because I was tired.

He stayed with me while I waited for the elevator. When it arrived, he took my hand, raised it to his lips, kissed it and murmured, "Thank you, Dina."

As I prepared for bed, I could still feel Eric's kiss on my hand.

I'd been wrong to spend so much time with him. Not that I was worried about what I'd felt when he put his arms around me at Sabrata: experience had shown me how misleading physical attraction could be. But I'd disregarded the intimate understanding that had existed between us in the past. It had gradually returned during the day, even when we were talking of only commonplace things, and I now realized it could be dangerous.

It should have been Philippe who occupied most of my thoughts. But since my arrival in Tripoli, Eric had been on my mind too often.

It would have been wise to avoid him, but how could I when we were both staying in the same hotel? My best defense was Philippe ... provided he didn't stay away too much longer. To reaffirm my feelings for him, it was urgent for me to see him again very soon.

THE FOLLOWING DAY I was all the more determined to resume my search because Eric had tried to discourage me. If he wanted me to stop searching, it was probably because there was something to discover.

I didn't want to call Philippe's company in Zelten, but there was no reason I shouldn't write to him there. I was sorry I hadn't thought of it sooner.

If I'd followed my inclination, my letter would have expressed more rancor than anxiety. I had to rewrite it several times before I managed to give it the same affectionate tone as the letters I'd written to him from France. I sent it special delivery.

One source of information that I hadn't completely exploited was the apartment Philippe had
rented. The owner of the building would know
when Philippe had canceled his lease, but first I had
to find out who the owner was. I went to Balatra
Street.

Luck was with me. In the entrance hall I met an
old Italian woman who, judging from the bag she
carried, was on her way out to do some shopping. I
told her I was looking for an apartment and asked if
she knew where I should inquire. From the wealth
of unnecessary details she lavished upon me, I
managed to glean that the building belonged to a
company, that the manager's office was nearby, and
that there were some vacant apartments, though
they were expensive.

"Everything is expensive here," she concluded
with a fatalistic sigh.

I wrote down the manager's name and address
and hurried away.

My conversation with the manager, a Libyan, was
brief. He told me that Philippe's lease hadn't been
canceled and that, as far as he knew, he still
occupied apartment number three on the seventh
floor, the one where I'd been given such a brusque
reception. When I remembered the small blond
Frenchwoman and her hostile look, an unpleasant
idea entered my mind. I didn't linger over it.
Philippe might have sublet the apartment without
notifying the manager.

I returned to the building. On the seventh floor, I read the name on the card tacked to the door: Marceline Lafont. I wasn't going to let her get off so easily this time.

When she opened the door, I stepped forward and blocked it with my foot, to keep her from closing it in my face. She opened her mouth to protest but I cut her short.

"Excuse me, but I must talk to you."

We sized each other up like a pair of combatants, though I had nothing against her. She seemed older than I'd thought the first time. Her face was drawn and there were dark rings around her eyes.

"What do you want?" she asked.

"I am looking for my fiancé, Philippe Cottens. There's no use saying you don't know him, since the apartment is rented in his name."

When she heard the word "fiancé," an ambiguous smile relaxed her pale lips.

"You're wasting your time if you think you're going to find him here."

"Have you seen him recently?"

"No."

"When did he sublet the apartment to you?"

She paused before answering.

"I've been living here several months. I don't think he's even in Libya any more."

"He was here last week, when he asked me to come."

She couldn't have looked more bewildered if I'd spoken in Greek.

"He asked you to come to Tripoli? Are you sure?"

"Of course. Otherwise I wouldn't be here."

"Well, I. . . . What can I say? I was sure he'd gone back to France. I may be mistaken. I don't really know him very well."

"If you have any information about him, I'd—"

"I don't want to get mixed up in it," she interrupted. "I have enough problems already!"

She grasped my shoulder and shoved me into the hallway. I didn't resist: I had no right to force my way into her apartment. She closed the door immediately and I heard her bolt it from the inside. I had no choice but to leave.

She obviously hadn't told me everything she knew, but she had given me an idea. I was convinced that Philippe hadn't left Libya and I thought I knew a way to make sure.

The office of the Transtourist Agency was on Istiklal Avenue. I began walking there rapidly. When I slowed to cross a street I heard footsteps behind me. I turned around and recognized the inevitable young Arab. He smiled pleasantly, as if we were old friends. This time I was so angry that I forgot to be afraid.

"What do you want from me?" I demanded.

"Nothing, mademoiselle."

"I can't go anywhere without finding you there. It's exasperating!"

"I don't do it on purpose. It's only by chance. Tripoli isn't a very big city."

"Yesterday you were outside of Tripoli, in the Giumia market."

"Everyone goes there. I'm Tunisian, and I'm a tourist here, like you. It's not surprising that we sometimes go to the same places."

His nationality explained why he spoke fluent French, and it was quite possible that he really was an innocent tourist. Had I been letting my imagination run away with me?

"My name is Taoufik Djelloud," he went on. "Will you remember that? We'll see each other again, and if you find yourself in any sort of difficulty, don't hesitate to call on me for help."

I had the feeling he was making fun of me. Before I could say so, he walked away.

At the Transtourist Agency, the Italian clerk behind the counter asked me if I was satisfied with my stay in Tripoli. I told her I had no complaints about my accommodations.

"You don't use our taxi very often," she said. "Has Musa done anything to offend you?"

"No, Musa is very nice, but I don't have much need for a car. Can you tell me when my hotel room was reserved for me?"

"A week before you arrived."

"Were you the one who talked with Philippe Cottens when he came to the agency?"

"He didn't come here. He made the arrangements

by telephone, and the next day he sent us the money to cover your expenses."

Why had Philippe used a travel agency to reserve a room in a hotel where he was already a guest? It didn't make sense.

Seeing my perplexed expression, the clerk asked anxiously, "Is anything wrong?"

"I was supposed to meet him in Tripoli but he's not here, and I'm wondering if perhaps he went to France. Maybe there was some confusion about the date."

"I don't think so. You arrived exactly when he told us you would."

"Even so, I'd like to find out if he took a plane or a ship out of Libya. Is that possible?"

"I'll check with the airlines and steamship companies, then I'll call you. Will you be at your hotel this afternoon?"

"Yes."

"I'll call you there as soon as I have anything to report."

At the hotel, the desk clerk told me that my mother had telephoned from Paris and wanted me to return her call. I decided to postpone it for a while. At this point it would be difficult to think of a plausible lie, and if I told my parents the truth they'd beg me to come home. I didn't want to worry them, but I also didn't want to leave without seeing Philippe.

When I went downstairs for lunch, Eric wasn't there. I felt a sense of relief.

Later, when I'd been reading in my room for an hour or so, the woman at the travel agency called to tell me that Philippe's name wasn't on the passenger lists of any airline or steamship company.

"They sent me copies of their lists for every day since the time he asked us to reserve a hotel room for you," she said. "Would you like me to try to find out if he crossed the border by bus or train?"

"No, that won't be necessary."

I thanked her and hung up. If Philippe hadn't gone back to France, I was sure he was still in Libya. I'd never really doubted it anyway.

Chapter 6

At dinnertime, Eric was waiting for me in the hotel restaurant.

"I thought you worked in the desert," I said to him. "How do you manage to be in Tripoli every night?"

"It's a long drive but it's worth it, to avoid sleeping in a tent. I prefer a comfortable hotel. You won't see me for the next two days, though. I have to go to Ghadames. Tell me what you did today. Did you discover anything new?"

"I found out that Philippe hasn't canceled the lease to the apartment he rented. There's a woman living in it now. He sublet it to her."

"Did you see her?"

"Yes, but she didn't tell me anything."

"Not even how she met Philippe?" he asked in a tone that made his implication clear.

"I can do without your insinuations," I said irritably.

"I'm not insinuating anything; I'm just making a natural assumption. When a woman moves into a man's apartment, it's reasonable to think that they're ... good friends."

"Not all men are like you."

"Will you please explain why it is that when a man is boring, women always believe he's faithful?"

"Eric! I trust Philippe and what you're saying is stupid!"

I made an effort to control my anger. I could see the kind of mood Eric was in and I didn't want to quarrel with him.

"Where else did you go?" he asked.

"To the Transtourist Agency. I wanted to make sure he hadn't left Libya."

Eric's face froze and I saw apprehension in his eyes.

"Well?"

"His name wasn't on any passenger list."

"What made you think he might have left the country?"

"Marceline Lafont, the woman in his apartment, said—What's the matter?"

He'd turned so pale that I thought he was sick, but he answered impatiently, "Nothing's the matter. What did she say?"

"She thought he'd gone back to France."

"And ... that was all ?"

"Yes."

I was struck by his expression of relief.

"What were you afraid she'd tell me ?" I asked.

"Afraid ? Don't be silly. I don't even know her. Are you still going to keep on waiting for Philippe ?"

"Certainly."

He dropped the subject and I was perfectly willing to let him.

When we finished dinner he asked, "Would you like to come for a drive ?"

The restaurant's floor show was about to begin. Having no interest in seeing another performance by the clumsy magician, I accepted Eric's invitation.

We took the road that ran along the coast. As soon as we had left the suburbs, he parked the car facing the sea. We were alone, the only sounds the breaking of the surf and the wind in the palms.

The roof of the car was open. Tilting back my head, I saw myriads of stars, more than I'd ever seen before. They were so dense that they merged into a kind of luminous mist.

Eric's voice drew me out of my contemplation.

"You're not afraid ?"

"If I were in danger, wouldn't you protect me ?"

"What if I were the danger ?"

I was about to laugh but he didn't give me a chance. He suddenly pulled me toward him and his lips pressed against mine. Seized with a kind of dizziness, I abandoned myself to his kiss. When I realized what I was doing, I violently pushed him away.

"Stop! You have no right to do that!"

My protest came too late, but it freed me from my weakness. I was so overwrought that my first impulse was to run away. I made a move to open the door; he stopped me.

"Don't be a fool. I don't mean to upset you."

My inner turmoil gave way to anger. I was furious with him and even more furious with myself.

"You have a strange way of showing it!" I retorted, barely able to control myself.

"Maybe, but now you know how dangerous Tripoli is at night."

"That kind of danger doesn't exist only in Tripoli! You haven't changed. You told me yourself that you're in love with someone else, and yet. . . ."

"Did I say that? I don't remember it."

"It doesn't matter. As far as I'm concerned, what does matter is that I'm engaged!"

"Ah, yes, to good old Philippe. Do you like the way he kisses you?"

"I don't want to talk to you any more! Take me back to the hotel!"

"As you wish."

He started the car and began slowly driving back toward the city.

I leaned against the door, sitting as far away from him as I could. What had happened to me? Had the starry night cast a spell on me, or was it simply that

Eric's kiss had affected me so deeply that it briefly made me forget our breakup, my engagement and the years that had passed since the last time he'd kissed me?

He began humming. I recognized the melody: we'd once heard that song together, and with romantic sentimentality we'd adopted it as "our song."

"Can't you sing something else?"

"You don't like that song?"

"I don't like the fact that you chose to sing it."

"I didn't choose to. It just happened to be running through my mind, that's all. I didn't know it had any special meaning for you."

I knew he was lying but I said nothing. He'd scored another point by more or less making me admit I remembered the song and what it had meant to us. We were both silent during the rest of the drive.

He parked near the hotel and opened the car door for me.

"Will you forgive me for upsetting you?" he asked as I climbed out.

He stood in front of me, looking at me with a faintly mocking smile. He was so sure of himself! What had he wanted to prove by that kiss? That he could make me forget Philippe if he wanted to? Surely he knew better than to draw such a conclusion from my moment of weakness, even if it had bolstered his ego.

He'd put me in an impossible situation, but I wasn't going to give him the satisfaction of admitting it.

"You had no right to kiss me," I answered, "but I forgive you for it."

He walked me to the door of the hotel, then said good night and went back to his car, without saying where he was going. Not that I wanted to know.

I went up to my room and sat in front of the window for a long time, thinking. I was glad Eric's work would keep him away for the next two days, and I hoped I wouldn't be alone with him again. Maybe Philippe would return before those two days were over.

Although I didn't attach any great importance to the incident in Eric's car, I couldn't deny that I was beginning to question my feelings for Philippe. It was becoming harder and harder for me not to believe that he'd abandoned me. I doubted him and I doubted myself.

For the first time, I suddenly had an urge to go back to France without clearing up the mystery. But I knew I wouldn't do it. Philippe had asked me to wait for him and I still felt I owed him a chance to justify himself.

ON SUNDAY I attended mass. As I was coming out of the cathedral I encountered Arnelli and his wife. I invited Signora Arnelli to have tea with me that afternoon at the Hotel Uaddan. My motive wasn't purely social: knowing how talkative she was, I hoped she might tell me something useful if her husband wasn't there to hold her in check.

It was such a beautiful day that I began walking with no particular destination in mind. Then, when I realized I was approaching Balatra Street, I suddenly decided to pay Marceline Lafont another visit. I hadn't planned it in advance but it now seemed of utmost importance. I remembered Eric's anxiety when I told him I'd talked to her and his relief when he learned that she hadn't given me any information about Philippe. Judging from his reaction, he was aware that she knew something important. I had to find out what it was.

To my surprise, the door of the apartment was opened by the old Italian woman I'd met in the entrance hall of the building the previous day.

"Is Marceline here?" I asked.

"Yes. Come in." She led me into the living room. "Have a seat. I'll tell her you're here."

I glanced around the room, and my attention was immediately caught by a photograph in a silver frame. It was a picture of Philippe. Stepping closer I saw that it was inscribed with the words: "For darling Marceline." It was in his handwriting.

I still hadn't recovered my presence of mind when Marceline came in. She was livid, but I could have sworn there was fear in her eyes.

I pointed to the photograph.

"And you told me you hardly knew him!"

"Just a minute."

She went to the door with the old Italian woman and came back alone.

"She does housework for me," she explained. "I told her to stop for today and come back tomorrow. I didn't want to talk in front of her."

"That picture has already told me more than enough!"

"You haven't read everything that's written on it."

She took the photograph out of its frame, turned it over and showed me the date on the back of it.

"As you can see," she said, "it was given to me three years ago. Before your engagement. You took him away from me."

"And you came to Tripoli to get him back."

"I'm a nurse. I work here."

"That doesn't answer my question. Did you know Philippe was here when you came?"

"Yes. I wanted to see him again, it's true, but I'm sorry now, believe me."

She seemed increasingly nervous. But I had no intention of making a jealous scene.

"Where is he?"

"I don't know. I've already told you that. The last time I saw him was two weeks ago. We'd had a quarrel a month before then. He wanted to make up. He came here like a thief. . . ."

She put her clenched fist over her mouth as though to stop herself from saying anything more.

"Why do you say 'like a thief'?"

"Because he robbed me."

This struck me as so ridiculous that I wondered if she was completely sane. If it hadn't been for the photograph I might have thought she was a pathological liar. I refrained from questioning her about the alleged robbery and tried to bring her back to reality.

"He didn't tell you where he was going?"

"That's the last thing he'd have told me! But I assure you there's no use looking for him in Libya. He's left the country."

"He was here last Tuesday."

A glow of hope relaxed her anxious face.

"You saw him then?"

"No, but he wrote to ask me to wait for him."

His note was in my purse. I showed it to her.

"That's his writing," she acknowledged. "I don't understand. I was sure he'd gone away for good. Listen to me. There's no longer anything between Philippe and me. Please don't come here again. It wouldn't do you any good, and it might do me harm."

"You won't help me to find him?"

"Even if I could, I wouldn't. My only advice to you is not to stay in Tripoli. Get out before it's too late."

She was becoming more and more nervous and distraught. I decided it would be pointless to try to find out anything further from her because she was in no condition to carry on a rational conversation.

As I turned to leave she said abruptly, "Go to see Saad ben Ibrahim Abed. He and Philippe were on very close terms."

"Where does he live?"

"On Grama Fresgleem Street."

I took out my notebook and jotted down the name and address. When I finished, she added, "If you see him, tell him that Philippe is a thief and that I have nothing in common with him any more. Nothing at all."

I WANDERED through the sundrenched streets until I reached the waterfront, where I sagged onto a bench, feeling dazed and bewildered. The photograph and its dedication, Marceline's incoherent words, her fear.... I began to wonder if I hadn't dreamed all that.

The sea was still blue and the sky was as clear as ever. I felt a little reassured by that placid reality.

Not far away I noticed Taoufik, the Tunisian, gazing out over the harbor. His stubborn surveillance seemed less upsetting to me than what I'd just learned. Philippe was unfaithful to me! I could hardly bring myself to believe it.

Even though he'd known Marceline before our engagement, it was apparent that they'd taken up with each other again, to the point where she'd moved into his apartment. Like Eric, Philippe had betrayed me. I should have been hurt, but mainly I was astounded. I'd trusted Philippe so much that I

still didn't want to judge him without having heard
what he had to say for himself.

I was determined to treat him more fairly than I'd
treated Eric. This time fairness would be easier for
me, since I was much less strongly affected by his
betrayal than I'd been by Eric's. From the start, I'd
been aware of the vast difference between my
affection for Philippe and the ardent, boundless
passion I'd felt for Eric. I'd wait to hear Philippe's
explanation before making any decision. To be
honest, I was secretly hoping he'd turn out to be
guilty, because I'd then be free to break our
engagement with a clear conscience.

I was suddenly ashamed of that feeling. I told
myself that appearances could be deceptive. Maybe
Marceline was a mentally unbalanced woman
whom Philippe had helped out of pity, and maybe
the fact that he hadn't told me about her only
showed his modesty in not wanting to brag about his
kindness.

I recalled her accusation of robbery and became
convinced that I ought to be highly skeptical of
everything she said. Anyone who knew Philippe
would laugh at hearing him called a thief. As for her
advice that I leave Tripoli immediately, I couldn't
take it seriously. But what about Saad Abed, the
man she claimed was a close friend of Philippe's? I
wondered if I should go to see him. I was no longer
very sure I really wanted to find out where Philippe
was.

A few hours later, when I'd gone back to the hotel and spent more time mulling over everything I'd learned, my indecision vanished. I had to clear things up with Philippe, once and for all. Trying to put it off would be childish. Since I had a lead, I would follow it up and see where it took me. I was about to leave my room and go to see Saad Abed when the desk clerk called to say that Signora Arnelli was waiting for me in the lobby. I'd forgotten my invitation, and now I hurried down to meet her.

As soon as we were having tea together, I realized how right I'd been to count on her indiscretion. After my visit that morning, I hesitated bringing up the subject of Marceline; it turned out that I didn't have to.

"You still haven't found out anything about your fiancé?" she asked.

"No, not really."

"Did you know he rented an apartment?"

"Well, I. . . ."

"I think you should go there. It's on Balatra Street. A friend of his is living in it now—a woman. Maybe she can tell you something useful."

I pretended to be ignorant.

"Who is she?"

"Her name is Marceline Lafont and she's a nurse. She had no trouble finding work here. Only a few days ago the government announced job openings for three hundred doctors and a hundred and fifty nurses, so—"

Not wanting her to wander from the subject, I interrupted her. "Did she know Philippe before she came here?"

"I've heard she's known him a long time. But don't be upset. She's not a rival, even though she used to have illusions."

"What kind of illusions?"

"There were rumors that she and Philippe were to be married. I don't know if she started those rumors herself, but I do know she did nothing to stop them. That's why we were so surprised when you arrived. We didn't know Philippe was engaged to someone in France."

"So you wondered which of us he was really engaged to?" I was beginning to wonder myself.

"No, it wasn't that. No one believed he was going to marry Marceline. It was obviously just wishful thinking on her part. Otherwise I wouldn't have told you about her."

"You were right to tell me."

"I thought it would be better for you to hear the truth from me, rather than getting a distorted version of the facts from gossip."

I restrained a smile. If it hadn't been for Signora Arnelli, I wouldn't have heard much gossip in Tripoli.

"I've already been to see Marceline Lafont."

"Really? Then there was no need for me to—"

"No, I'm glad you told me what you did, because she wasn't very helpful. She seemed terrified. Would you know why?"

"I don't know of any reason she should be terrified. YOu must have been mistaken."

I knew I wasn't. Marceline's fear had been obvious. But I dropped the subject and asked, "Do you know a man named Saad ben Ibrahim Abed?"

My question dumbfounded her for a moment but she quickly recovered.

"Saad Abed? Who told you about him?"

"Marceline said he was a friend of Philippe's."

"So that's it! She's jealous. You mustn't pay any attention to what she says."

"What do you mean, 'jealous'?"

"Abed has a sister who's said to be very beautiful. She lives with him. Although she's always veiled when she goes out, in his house she wears European clothes and no veil. Philippe admired her, but it's nothing for you to worry about."

I wasn't worried, in spite of the Marceline episode, because I didn't think Philippe was fickle enough to have *two* other women.

"Who is Saad Abed?"

"A former camel driver who's become enormously rich. Things like that happen in this country, because of oil. It generates such colossal amounts of money that a lot of it stays in the hands of middlemen. In the past ten years many people have made huge fortunes, in ways that aren't always publicly known. Abed's success has gone to his head, and there are horrifying rumors about him. It would be a serious mistake to cross him in any way. I think you'd better stay away from him."

I told her I had no desire to antagonize Saad Abed and thanked her for her information.

So it had taken me days to discover what everyone in Tripoli apparently knew: that Philippe had resumed an old romance with Marceline and that it had seemed serious enough to create the impression that they were going to be married.

Eric must have known about it, too. Why hadn't he told me? Was he afraid I'd think he was telling me because he was jealous? No, it couldn't be that, since he was in love with someone else. Maybe he just couldn't bear to tell me something that would be so painful to me. But had it really caused me very much pain?

Chapter 7

When a call came through for me from Zelten, I hoped I was about to talk with Philippe at last. Instead, it was a secretary who told me that my special-delivery letter had reached the company but that it couldn't be delivered because M. Cottens no longer worked for the E.R.P.C.

"What!" I exclaimed. "When did he leave the company?"

"At the beginning of the month. He didn't give us a forwarding address, so all we can do is send the letter back to you. Since you sent it special delivery, I thought it might be urgent, so I decided to call you in case it was important for you to know as soon as possible that your letter hadn't reached Monsieur Cottens."

"Thank you very much. I appreciate it."

I slowly replaced the receiver. I was more shaken

by the news of Philippe's resignation than I'd been
by the discovery of Marceline's existence. It made
his behavior even more incomprehensible. Since
there was no longer any reason for him to be in
Libya, why had he asked me to come there? Had he
found another job? If so, where? And why hadn't he
told me about it?

So far, all my efforts to find him had failed. There
was only one thing left for me to do: I must see Saad
Abed.

I telephoned his house. A maid answered and
informed me I couldn't make an appointment with
him unless I first wrote a letter explaining my
reasons for wanting to see him. I kept insisting till
she finally agreed to ask him if he would make an
exception in my case. When she came back to the
telephone she said he would see me at four o'clock.

The sky had been cloudy all morning but the city
was again glittering in sunlight by the time Musa
came for me.

When I told him the address, he forgot his usual
reserve and asked, "You're going to see Saad Abed?"

"Yes. I didn't expect you to recognize his address."

"I know Tripoli very well."

After driving a few minutes, Musa stopped at a
service station.

"It'll only take a moment. I need to get some gas."

He went inside the station while the attendant
pumped the gas. I noticed that it took only a very

small amount to fill the tank, but I said nothing about this to Musa when he came back to the car.

Twenty minutes later we stopped in front of an imposing three-story house surrounded by an immense garden.

I was early, so when a servant led me into a luxurious drawing room I had time to admire the furniture and paintings. Then the door opened and Abed entered. A rather fat man of average height, he appeared to be in his mid-forties. He bowed politely.

"You've come to talk about Philippe?" he asked in Italian. "Where is he?"

My disappointment made me stammer.

"But I.... That's ... that's what I came here to ask you."

"He didn't send you? Then who told you to see me?"

"Marceline Lafont."

I told him why I'd come to Tripoli, then described my efforts to find Philippe and my conversation with Marceline, though I didn't repeat her accusation that Philippe had robbed her. Abed listened with interest and surprise. He watched me closely, his eyes suspicious and crafty. I was sure Signora Arnelli had been right to warn me to be careful not to cross him.

"I'll be frank with you," he said. "I saw Philippe quite often for six months or so, and he never said a word to me about you. I thought he was engaged to

Marceline Lafont, till he left his apartment and
went to stay at the Hotel Uaddan."

"You have no idea where he might be now ?"

"I did have an idea, but what you've just told me
changes everything. I'd like to find him, too. We
have certain business matters to settle. I've looked
for him everywhere. I even called Zelten."

"He doesn't work for the E.R.P.C. any more."

"You knew he'd been fired ?"

"Fired ? That's impossible!"

I'd automatically assumed that he'd resigned. It
would never have occurred to me that Philippe, so
conscientious and efficient, might have been dismissed by the company that had employed him for
years.

"No, it's not impossible. I have enough connec-
tions in the oil companies, including the E.R.P.C., to
know what I'm talking about. He was fired."

"Why ?"

"I don't know. I haven't seen him since it
happened."

"But aren't you his friend ?"

"That's putting it a bit strongly. He and I don't
have the same idea of friendship."

From the way he said this, it was clear that for
some reason he had a grudge against Philippe. I
realized he wasn't going to be my ally and that I'd
gain nothing by continuing our conversation. Before
leaving I asked him, only for the sake of form, to let

me know if anything new came to light on Philippe's whereabouts.

That evening Eric, back from Ghadames, joined me in the hotel restaurant. I had so many questions to ask him that I scarcely knew where to begin. He solved the problem by questioning me first.

"Why did you go to see Saad Abed?"

"Who told you I did?"

"It doesn't matter. You have to stop being so reckless, Dina. Abed is a dangerous man."

"You're exaggerating again."

"No, I'm not exaggerating. He's rich, powerful, unscrupulous and merciless. Why did you see him?"

"Marceline Lafont told me he was Philippe's friend."

"She must be out of her mind! Everyone knows that Philippe and Abed are on bad terms with each other now."

This statement showed that, no matter what he said, Eric knew more about Philippe's life than he'd told me.

"It's clear to me that I could have spared myself a lot of trouble if you'd been more honest with me. Don't you think it's time you stopped hiding things?"

He looked at me with his eyes half-closed.

"What do you think I should have told you?"

"What you know about Philippe."

"For example?"

The first thing that came into my mind was Philippe's relationship with Marceline, but I didn't want to discuss that with Eric.

"For example, that he'd stopped working for the E.R.P.C."

"If I'd told you that he was fired for ... lack of integrity, would you have believed me ?"

"What a ridiculous idea !"

"You see ! I can't tell you anything. You refuse to listen."

Although unconvinced and skeptical, I still wanted to hear what he had to say.

"I'll listen now. Tell me what happened."

"To begin with I'll only be repeating what I've heard, though it seems to be common knowledge all over Tripoli. I haven't checked on it myself. Do you know how oil concessions are granted ?"

"Not really."

"In exchange for payment of royalties, the government gives a company the right to prospect for oil in a certain territory for a certain period of time, usually eight years. Every two years the company must give back a quarter of the concession—any quarter it chooses. That territory is then turned over to a rival company."

"The first company always chooses the worst part of its concession, doesn't it ?"

"Of course."

"Then why would another company want it ?"

"Prospecting methods are constantly being improved. For example, some of the richest deposits were discovered in territories that had been given up by eight different companies. So choosing which part of a concession to give up is a very important matter. For the E.R.P.C., the decision depended partly on reports drawn up by Philippe. You can guess the rest."

"Don't make me guess. Tell me."

"Following Philippe's advice, the company turned over a piece of land where a huge deposit was discovered two months later."

"Well, what of it? Anyone can make a mistake."

The company didn't see it that way. Who told you Philippe had been fired?"

"Abed. But he didn't say why."

Eric laughed.

"I think he could have told you if he'd wanted to. The rival company, the one that found the oil, is supposed to have won the concession through his efforts."

I remembered Abed saying that he had "certain business matters" to settle with Philippe. Was he referring to sharing a bribe?

"It's still hard to accept your story," I said.

"It's not 'my' story. I knew Philippe was no longer with the E.R.P.C., but it wasn't until yesterday that I heard that explanation, true or false, for his departure."

"You think it's true?"

"There's so much money involved in the oil

business that it's easy to be tempted. Yes, I think it's true, though that's only my personal opinion. Is there anything else you want to ask me?"

"Yes. What is there between Philippe and Saad Abed?"

"You won't like what I have to say...."

"Don't worry about whether I'll like it or not."

"All right, but again I must tell you that there are some things I don't know for certain. Abed has a sister who's engaged to a man from one of the most influential families in Libya. Her marriage will be very useful to him ... if it ever takes place."

"Is there something that may prevent it?"

"Abed made the mistake of introducing his sister to Philippe, and she fell in love with him. With the complicity of one of the maids, she managed to slip out of the house several times to see him."

This time I was the one who laughed.

"So, according to you, Philippe is a real Don Juan!"

"There's no need to be a Don Juan to capture the fancy of a young woman who leads a secluded life, cut off from the world."

"She's not completely cut off from the world. I've heard that she's emancipated enough to wear European clothes at home, which must mean that her brother's friends see her without a veil."

"I see someone has already told you about her. But you apparently don't know that she and her brother are Tuaregs. Among the Tuaregs—or at least among

those who still live in the old traditional way—it's
the men who are veiled, not the women. The fact is
that she was *kept* in strict seclusion, especially since
her marriage would be such an advantage to Abed."

"For a former camel driver. . . ."

"He was never a camel driver; that's a myth. He
started out as a bank clerk."

"I can understand his ambition, but I don't see
how his sister's marriage could be put in danger by a
few meetings with Philippe."

"That only shows you don't know how Arab men
feel about such things. Anything else you want to
ask me?"

I had no desire to hear him tell me about
Marceline.

"No. I'll save my other questions till I see
Philippe."

Eric's face took on a look of sadness.

"You insisted that I tell you what I know, and
now you resent me for it."

"You haven't told me anything. You've repeated a
lot of gossip, and you've enjoyed doing it. That's why
I resent you."

"You're being unfair, Dina!"

Maybe I *was* unfair. I couldn't deny that his
"gossip" tallied with things I'd learned from other
sources. If he'd told me all that when I first came to
Tripoli, I'd have regarded it as nothing but malicious
invention, but I couldn't believe that Signora

Arnelli, Marceline Lafont and Saad Abed had all
conspired to mislead me.

One thing was perplexing. What I'd found out in
Tripoli had destroyed my image of Philippe; yet I'd
come there only because he asked me to. Surely he
hadn't sent for me because he wanted me to discover
that he was unfaithful to me and had been fired
from his job for dishonesty! If he wanted to break
our engagement, there were less unpleasant and
expensive ways of doing it.

I was more determined than ever to find him
because I needed to know the truth, even though I
was beginning to fear it.

I RECEIVED two letters the next morning. One was
from my mother, saying that she was worried
because she hadn't heard from me. The other was in
Italian and unsigned. The handwriting was so
awkward that it was hard to read.

You are looking for Signor Cottens. I can tell you
where he is but I need money because I am poor.
Go to Leptis Magna tomorrow. I will be in the
ruins at two o'clock in the afternoon. Bring money
and tell no one about this letter. If you are not
alone, I will say nothing.

The envelope had a Tripoli postmark. Why had
the anonymous man—I assumed the letter was from
a man, judging by the handwriting—told me to meet

him in Leptis Magna, forty miles away? The whole thing seemed highly suspicious but I decided I hadn't much choice. I couldn't pass up a chance, no matter how slim, of finding out where Philippe was.

Naturally I had no intention of telling Eric about my plans. Thinking it would be better to avoid him completely, I had dinner brought to my room that evening.

When he called to ask why I hadn't come to the restaurant, I said I had a headache. He didn't believe me, but convinced I was avoiding him because I was angry with him, he made no comment.

THE NEXT DAY, I called for Musa to pick me up. When he arrived and was helping me into the car, I told him my destination for the day. Before climbing back in himself he hurried into the hotel saying he needed to cal his wife about something she wanted him to buy that day.

Soon we were on our way to Leptis Magna. In my purse was all the cash I had, one hundred fifty Libyan pounds. I was determined not to pay anything unless I received some solid information.

We drove east on the long coastal road that runs from Tunis to Cairo, and the countryside made me feel as if I'd slipped into Biblical times. Flocks of sheep were being tended by shepherds in flowing wool garments; veiled women drew water from wells; hobbled camels swayed majestically and little donkeys plodded along with heavy burdens.

When we reached Leptis Magna I was surprised to discover that the place was deserted. Remembering Sabrata, I'd expected to see at least a few tourists.

I left Musa at the entrance to the excavations and began walking along the shaded lane that led to the ruins, still without seeing another living soul.

My anonymous letter writer hadn't told me exactly where to meet him. Now that I saw what a vast area the ruins covered, that omission seemed strange. They weren't the remains of a small colonial town, but of a great city, with broad streets, spacious forums, majestic temples and countless other buildings.

I wandered at random, not knowing what else to do, hoping that sooner or later the man would approach me. Soon I reached an amphitheater and climbed to the top tier of seats. From there I could be seen from far away; it was an ideal place to wait if someone was looking for me.

The whole city was spread out before me; but it was a dead city, with no sign of motion anywhere. I saw only tall columns, dilapidated walls, empty temples, and farther off, the seashore, where the remains of docks lay beneath the foaming waves.

I stood there a long time, finally realizing that even if the man had seen me, he was unlikely to approach me in such a conspicuous place. At least I'd given him a chance to spot me. Maybe he was waiting nearby.

Finally I came down. As soon as I left the

amphitheater I became certain I was being followed.
I heard pebbles rolling and sometimes even distinct
footsteps, but in the mass of jumbled ruins it was
impossible to tell exactly where the sounds were
coming from. Several times I stopped and waited; no
one came to sight. I was beginning to lose patience
when I walked around the corner of a temple and
found myself facing an Arab dressed in European
clothes.

"Are you Geraldine Montanier?" he asked in
Italian.

He was short and nearly bald, and I couldn't
remember ever having seen him before. I'd believed
that the anonymous letter had been written by
someone I already knew and had particularly
suspected Taoufik Djelloud.

"You wanted to see me?" I asked cautiously.

"Yes."

"What do you have to tell me?"

"It's about Signor Cottens. But first give me the
money."

He was going a little too fast. I had no intention of
paying him in advance.

"Do you know where he is?"

"Pay me first."

"How much do you want?"

"Two hundred pounds."

"I don't have that much."

I tightened my grip on my purse. That seemed to
be the sign he was waiting for. He rushed at me,

grabbed the purse and took off at a run. I screamed, not thinking how pointless it was in that deserted place.

All at once the thief stopped: Eric had just stepped in front of him. I didn't have a chance to wonder what he was doing there for a moment later the two men began fighting with savage violence.

"Run away!" Eric shouted to me. "Run away!"

I couldn't have moved if I'd wanted to. I stood there, paralyzed, unable even to try to help Eric. Not that he seemed to need any help: twice he sent his adversary sprawling on the ground. But when he was knocked down a third time, the Arab picked up a stone and threw it at Eric, striking him on the forehead. Temporarily blinded by the blood that poured from his wound, Eric could scarcely stay on his feet.

The thief snatched up my purse, which he'd been forced to drop, and began running again. He didn't go far before he was blocked by Musa and Taoufik Djelloud.

While Musa held him, Taoufik hurried to Eric and asked, "Are you badly hurt?"

"No. Go back and help Musa. I don't want that man to get away."

Eric pulled out his handkerchief and pressed it against his wound, trying to stem the bleeding. I went up to him while Taoufik joined Musa and the thief.

"You know Taoufik and Musa?" I asked in bewilderment.

"Yes."

"But what . . . why are the three of you here?"

"We'll go into that later. First tell me why you're here."

I told him about the anonymous letter, expecting him to lecture me angrily on how foolish I'd been to take such a risk. But he merely nodded.

He went to the thief and had a long conversation with him, which I couldn't decipher. Finally Eric took out his wallet and handed him some money. A few seconds later the man walked away, escorted by Musa and Taoufik.

Eric came back to me, still pressing his handkerchief against his forehead. Blood had stained his shirt.

"You gave him money!" I exclaimed indignantly.

"He's a very poor man."

"He's a robber!"

"He has excuses. He and his family are hungry; they live in a miserable shack and he has no regular work."

"Are Musa and Taoufik going to turn him over to the police?"

"No. They're going to put him on a bus back to Tripoli."

"Does he know Philippe?"

"He's never laid eyes on him. Now and then he lands temporary work as a porter, and last week he

replaced one of the porters at the Hotel Uaddan. He
overheard your conversation with the desk clerk
when you arrived: you asked for someone named
Signor Cottens and seemed upset when you were
told that he was no longer at the hotel. He noticed
that you still seemed worried afterward, so he came
up with the idea of writing that letter. His plan was
to meet you here and steal your purse."

"Why here?"

"To give himself a better chance of getting away
without being caught by the police."

"What if I hadn't come?"

"He'd have gone back to Tripoli and his bus fare
would have been wasted. Come, we've stayed here
long enough."

We began walking. I was completely lost but he
seemed to know his way out of the ruins, so I
followed his lead.

"How did you know I was here? And who's
Taoufik?"

"Before asking me any more questions, you might
thank me."

"I'm overwhelmed with gratitude, but that
doesn't keep me from being puzzled."

"Taoufik is a friend of mine and...."

He stopped. His face suddenly turned pale and he
swayed unsteadily on his feet.

"What's the matter?" I asked anxiously.

"I'm dizzy. I think I'd better sit down."

His wound was worse than I'd thought. I helped

him to sit on the ground, knelt beside him and put my arms around him to support him.

"Do you feel better now?"

"I feel wonderful." He closed his eyes and murmured, "Dina . . . my darling."

I wondered if I'd heard right, then decided he must be a little delirious and was confusing the present with the past.

"You don't know what you're saying."

"My mind is perfectly clear. I've never loved anyone but you."

"But you told me—"

"I told you I'd loved only once in my life, and it's true. You're the only one I've ever loved."

"For God's sake, Eric—"

"I can't talk about it any more now. My head hurts."

Not without suspicion, I examined him. There was a huge swelling around the cut on his forehead. He was still pale and beads of sweat had appeared on his face. I could no longer question the seriousness of his condition. And he was undoubtedly delirious.

Musa and Taoufik came back. As soon as he saw Eric, Taoufik was horrified.

"It's all right. I'm over it now," said Eric, "but I have a terrible headache."

"We can see a doctor in Homs," suggested Taoufik.

"There's no need to stop there. I can make it back to Tripoli."

He stood up with a grimace and we began walking again. Taoufik suggested to Eric, "Why don't you ride in Musa's Mercedes? You'll be more comfortable. I'll drive your Fiat back for you."

Since that was obviously the most sensible suggestion Eric and I climbed into the back seat of the Mercedes while Musa started the engine.

"We can talk freely," Eric said to me, nodding toward Musa. "He doesn't understand French."

"What difference does it make? Are you going to tell me some secrets?"

"Who knows what I may tell you?"

I preferred not to answer.

On the way to Leptis Magna I hadn't paid any attention to the condition of the road. Now I realized how bad it was when I heard Eric swear with every jolt.

"It's like being hit with a sledgehammer," he grumbled.

"Do you want to lie down?"

"That would be worse. It's going to be a miserable ride no matter what I do, and I have you to thank for it!"

His reproach made me bristle. I hadn't asked him to follow me, much less get into a fight to recover my purse!

"You didn't have to stop that man. I'd rather have lost my purse."

"Is there much money in it?"

"A hundred and fifty pounds."

"That's worth a bump on the head."

I already regretted my irritation.

"It's a horrible bump," I sighed. "You're going to be sick for a while."

He took my hand and smiled. "Ah, but I've never felt better in my life."

I tried to pull my hand away but he held it firmly.

"It's not funny."

"Who's trying to be? If you only knew how unhappy I've been the last three years—"

"You're losing your mind!"

"I wish I could," he said, laughing, "because then my head would stop hurting. Dina, I didn't intend to tell you this so soon, but now that I've started you must listen to me. I've never stopped loving you. I still love you as much as ever, more than ever—"

"Either you're delirious or you're making fun of me. Either way, I wish you'd be quiet."

"I can't be quiet any longer. I love you, Dina. Don't you understand that?"

"And what about Philippe? You're forgetting him."

"He doesn't count; he's never counted. You agreed to marry him out of spite, to make me miserable."

He spoke feverishly. His eyes were shining and he gripped my hand so hard that he almost hurt me.

"You succeeded," he went on, "more than you know. You ... tortured me. When you broke our engagement I nearly lost my mind. Then you left Paris and didn't answer my letters. I went to your

apartment and begged your mother to tell me where
you were, so I could see you again, at least once. I
wept in front of her—yes, cried like a child. But it
had no effect on her. You'd have been proud to see
how well she followed your instructions."

My mother had never told me a word about his
visit. I could understand why : she was afraid I'd get
in touch with him and give in to his pleas. But I
regretted her silence.

"You're wrong, Eric, I didn't give her any
instructions, because I had no idea you'd come to see
her. And she never told me about the visit."

The joy that transformed his face seemed out of
proportion to what I'd just said.

"I knew it!" he exclaimed. "I knew it wasn't you!
Oh, Dina, if only I could have seen you again.
Afterward, I told myself I had to have the courage to
wait. I thought that if I gave you enough time, your
anger would die down and your attitude toward me
wouldn't be so unfair. When I was offered a job in
Morocco I took it and for months I hoped to hear
from you. But you never wrote. Finally I began
writing to you again."

I'd never received any letters. I was in England at
the time, and my mother had apparently thought it
would be best not to forward them to me.

"I was just about to go back to France, determined
to see you again no matter what happened, when I
heard about your engagement. I took the next plane

to Paris and went straight to your apartment. Again it was your mother who talked to me."

"What did she tell you?" I asked.

"She succeeded in convincing me that you'd forgotten me. She said you were very happy and that I'd meant nothing more to you than an adolescent flirtation. My hope of making you change your mind seemed so ridiculous to her that she nearly laughed in my face. By the time I finished talking to her, she'd completely destroyed any hopes I had.

"I decided to forget you, too. I met other women and tried to fall in love with some of them. But it was no use. You were going to marry someone else and I'd always be alone."

He suddenly bent forward and took his head between his hands as if he were trying to squeeze the pain out of it. I became alarmed.

"You're in no condition to get upset, Eric. Why don't you lean on me and rest for a while?"

He sat up with a smile, then put his head on my shoulder.

In the front seat, Musa continued to drive in silence. I sincerely hoped he really didn't understand French. I refused to think about what Eric had said to me, but his head was heavy on my shoulder, and as I looked out at the peaceful countryside I was remembering what it had been like to be happy.

Chapter 8

Eric consented to go to a doctor when we reached Tripoli. X rays showed no sign of fracture or serious concussion, so the doctor stitched it up and gave him some pills for the pain.

At dinner he had a bandage on his forehead when he joined me in the restaurant of the Hotel Uaddan. After talking with him a few moments I decided he'd recovered enough for me to ask him some questions that were still unanswered.

"Who is Taoufik Djelloud?"

"I've already told you: he's a friend of mine."

"Well, your friend has been following me ever since I came to Tripoli. Has he been spying on me for his own pleasure?"

"He's not spying on you; he's watching over you. I was once able to help him out of a tight scrape, so he's grateful to me. Also, we're friends. When you

118

came here, he was on vacation. I told him I was worried about your being alone in Tripoli and he offered to act as your bodyguard."

I felt a surge of irritation as I remembered my efforts to escape from that unwanted protector.

"What a brilliant idea! Did he tell you how I tried to get away from him?"

"Yes, and he was sorry he'd frightened you."

"I bet you had a good laugh about it! You should have told me what he was doing."

"I thought you might be angry. What are you reproaching me for, Dina? Being worried about you?"

"So when you asked me what I'd been doing, you always knew before I told you! Taoufik kept you posted on every move I made. But what about my trip to Leptis Magna? How did you know...."

I stopped short because I'd just realized the answer. Musa had called Taoufik when he went into the hotel with the excuse that he needed to call his wife. I should have known!

"And I thought Musa was a discreeet man!" I exclaimed.

"Don't be unfair. When Taoufik explained the situation to him, Musa volunteered to cooperate and refused to accept any money for it. He felt he was only doing his duty by helping to keep you out of trouble.

"This afternoon he called Taoufik to report that he was taking you to Leptis Magna, and Taoufik immediately notified me. I couldn't imagine why you were going there but I didn't like the idea of it. Taoufik and I decided to go after you. And while I'm on the subject, let me tell you how foolish you were. An anonymous letter—"

"Never mind the anonymous letter. It doesn't change the fact that you've been having me watched without my permission, and for no good reason. Philippe wouldn't have asked me to come to Tripoli if he'd thought I'd be in any danger."

Eric bowed his head and said without looking at me, "I don't know what Philippe thinks, but I'm worried about you because I love you."

"And he doesn't?"

He raised his head and looked me straight in the eyes.

"Haven't you understood yet, even now that you know about Marceline Lafont and Saad Abed's sister?"

"You knew he'd been living with Marceline?"

"Of course."

"Then why didn't you tell me?"

"I wasn't at all sure you'd believe me, and even if you did, you'd have resented me for destroying your illusions."

"At this point I don't have any illusions left. Both the men I've loved have been unfaithful to me."

"That's not true! First of all, you never loved Philippe, no matter what you say. And second, I wasn't unfaithful to you. If you'd—"

I interrupted him, not wanting to take up that old quarrel again.

"If Philippe has stopped loving me, why did he send for me and pay all my expenses in advance?"

Eric gave me such a strange look that for a moment I thought he was going to tell me something else he'd held back till now; but then he seemed to change his mind.

"I didn't know he'd paid your expenses in advance. Who knows why? But his feelings don't matter: what matters is that you've never loved him. You may have tried to convince yourself you did, but you always knew in your heart that it wasn't true. I shouldn't have listened to your mother. I was so blind! Why didn't I go and insist that you break that ridiculous engagement! When I think that I almost lost you. . . ."

He was so upset that he began to shake. The injury and his emotional state combined to make him easily distraught. I tried to remain levelheaded but, for the first time, I really believed he still loved me, and that realization dazzled me.

"Be calm, Eric. I understand what you're saying, but there's still Philippe. I can't decide anything till I've seen and talked with him. I have to clear things up between us. Then I'll have a right to ask myself how I feel about you."

He took my hand and smiled.

"I'll wait, Dina. I already know your feelings, and I'm happy."

I was happy, too. But, alone in my room I analyzed my joy and discovered how fragile it was.

Even if Eric was right in saying I'd never stopped loving him, it was still true that one of my reasons for breaking our engagement was that I regarded marrying him as a very risky prospect. Philippe, on the other hand, had seemed a safe, sensible choice. Now he, too, had disappointed me, but did that make marriage with Eric any less risky?

Fully aware of the physical attraction he exercised, I found it hard to think clearly around Eric. If I wanted to decide my future in a calm, rational frame of mind, I had to get away from him for a time, and that was only possible if I returned to France.

It would mean giving up my efforts to find Philippe and leaving without knowing why I'd come. But was I really waiting for him out of loyalty, or because I didn't want to leave Eric?

Philippe couldn't expect me to be patient any longer. If he still wanted to see me, he could rejoin me in Paris.

But it wasn't easy to resign myself to leaving without seeing Eric again. I knew he was about to go back to Ghadames for several days. I'd write to him and he'd understand why a separation was important for both of us.

I went to bed with my mind firmly made up.

THE NEXT DAY, my determination was weakening. I left the hotel, but instead of going to the Transtourist

Agency to buy a plane ticket to Paris, as I'd intended, I began wandering aimlessly through the streets and parks, thinking about everything that Eric had said to me and struggling against my desire to stay in Tripoli.

Propriety finally tipped the balance in favor of leaving. Philippe was paying all my expenses in Tripoli; now that I seriously doubted our engagement would continue, I didn't feel right about accepting his help.

Early the following morning I went to the Transtourist Agency. All flights to Paris were booked solid for the next three days, so I took the earliest reservation I could get.

Leaving the agency I encountered Taoufik, for the first time since Eric's injury.

"Here you are! I was beginning to think you'd given up watching me."

He smiled broadly.

"Eric would never forgive me if I did."

"I didn't see you yesterday."

"Maybe not, but I was there. I followed you everywhere."

"You must have been wearing a veil."

The very idea made him laugh. I laughed with him. Now that I was no longer afraid of him, I found him quite likable.

"You're making progress in keeping out of sight," I said, "but it won't be useful to you much longer. I'm leaving Tuesday."

This news seemed to throw him into consternation.

"Does Eric know?"

"Not yet."

"You're not going to wait for him? He'll be back on Thursday."

"I'm taking a flight to Paris Tuesday morning."

"Why so soon? You're not enjoying your stay in Tripoli?"

"I have to go home. In the meantime, why don't you walk to the hotel with me, rather than trailing along behind me? We may as well keep each other company."

It was the first time I'd had a chance to talk with Taoufik. I asked him about his family and his country, Tunisia. Although he answered me unhesitatingly it was easy to see that his mind was elsewhere. When he left me at the door of the hotel, I was sure he would try to get in touch with Eric and tell him about my plans.

After lunch, to kill time, I went to the hairdressing salon in the hotel and spent two hours there. When I returned to my room, there was a telegram on my table. I opened it, convinced it was from Eric, but I was mistaken.

Forgive my silence and be patient a little longer. I will explain everything.

                                        Philippe

It had been sent from Yeffren that afternoon. I looked for that name on the map the agency had given me and discovered it at the edge of the large yellow area representing the Libyan Desert. It was about a two-hour drive from Tripoli.

There was no reason to assume that Philippe was still there. He might have left, or maybe he'd only stopped in the town to send his telegram. Even so, I would have gone there immediately if it hadn't been so late in the day. I didn't like the idea of arriving in a strange town after dark, without knowing how to go about finding out if Philippe was there or not.

That telegram changed everything. Just as I was about to go back to Paris and forget Philippe, he'd reminded me that I'd come to Tripoli for the express purpose of seeing him. He was still thinking of me.

I called the Transtourist Agency, canceled my plane reservation and asked to have Musa come by for me the next day.

I was about to go to bed when Eric called. Sure enough, Taoufik had told him I intended to leave on Tuesday.

"I've changed my plans," I told him. "I want to see the desert before I leave."

"You want to go to Ghadames?"

"No, Yeffren will be good enough."

There was a silence at the other end of the line; then Eric said in an odd tone, "Yeffren? You're going to Yeffren?"

He sounded as if he was trying to keep from laughing.

"That's right, I'm going to Yeffren. What's so funny about that?"

"When?"

"Tomorrow."

"How?"

"Musa will drive me."

"I have a better idea: I'll take you there."

"But I've already asked the agency to send Musa."

"I'll call them in the morning and say you won't need him. Meet me in the hotel restaurant at nine and we'll leave as soon as we've finished breakfast. How does that suit you?"

I knew I ought to refuse but I heard myself answer, "I suppose it's. . . . All right, I'll be there."

I wondered if he would have been so eager to take me to Yeffren if he'd known why I wanted to go there.

ERIC WAS ALREADY waiting at a table when I entered the restaurant. He stood up and took both my hands.

"You wanted to leave me," he said reproachfully.

"I've already told you I changed my plans. But you seem to have changed yours, too. I thought you were supposed to be in Ghadames till Thursday."

"I was, but now it's been decided that I'll spend two weeks working in Tripoli, starting tomorrow."

"You don't have to work today?"

"No, I asked to have the day off."

"So you could be my chauffeur?"

"That wasn't what I had in mind when I made my request, but since you want to go to Yeffren, I'll drive you there. I'll take you on the standard guided tour: Gharian, the mountains, Yeffren, and a sample of the desert."

I didn't have the courage to say that only Yeffren interested me. Besides, I wasn't even sure it was true. With Eric, I was ready to go anywhere.

It was a beautiful day. I was beginning to think the Libyan weather was always perfect, but Eric told me that the heat was often unbearable in summer. Without knowing it, I'd come during the best season.

We were driving across a plain that extended to a blue line of mountains on the horizon. Here and there, sheep and black goats grazed on sparse grass.

We hadn't talked very much. Eric kept his eyes on the road, frowning slightly.

"Is anything wrong?" I asked.

"Why?"

"You look grim."

"It's just that the sun tires my eyes. I think I'd better put on my sunglasses. They're in the glove compartment. Will you please get them for me?"

I handed them to him, remarking, "Your eyes seem to be very sensitive to sunlight. The other day, in that seaside restaurant—"

"What a memory!"

The dark glasses hid his eyes but couldn't mask the tension in his face.

Before long we began driving up the first slope of the mountains. Now and then we passed a truck or a heavily laden donkey. The view broadened as we rose, the plain behind us seeming to stretch endlessly in every direction.

When we reached the summit, Eric stopped the car and we climbed out to admire the view. The air was cool and the wind whipped our faces. He put his arm around my shoulders and appeared much more relaxed.

Soon after we began driving again, his now almost cheerful mood began to make me more uneasy than his earlier preoccupation. What would happen if Philippe was in Yeffren? I should have gone there alone. How could I clear things up between Philippe and me if Eric was with us?

We passed through fertile valleys whose slopes enclosed little villages. At Gharian we stopped to visit an open-air market.

Then the road began winding among sand dunes carved into smooth, undulating shapes by the wind, studded with green patches of esparto grass.

"You wanted to see the desert," said Eric. "This isn't the middle of the vast Sahara, of course, and we don't have to worry about dying of thirst if our car breaks down, but there's still sand as far as the eye can see, esparto grass, dryness, blazing sunlight and nomads."

He pointed to black tents spread on the ground like gigantic bats, in groups of twos and threes. They were so far from the road that it was hard to make out the people around them. Eric told me how the Berbers fiercely guarded their precarious homes from the curiosity of strangers.

"The Tuaregs are more hospitable," he said. "At Ghadames, nearly a thousand of them are camped outside the town. Tuareg women don't wear veils and they're the freest of all Moslem women."

I thought of Saad Abed's sister.

"Are they pretty?"

"Why do you ask? Are you jealous of the mysterious Meryem?"

"That's the name of Abed's sister?"

"So I've heard."

"What else have you heard about her?"

"Look, there's an oasis." He pointed to a shallow gully surrounded by palm trees. "Did you know that the population of the Sahara will soon reach a million?"

I would have preferred to know why he suddenly decided not to say anything more about Abed's sister, but I didn't pursue the topic.

We caught sight of a promontory crowned with white houses. Eric announced that we were approaching Yeffren, and I began to feel apprehensive about what would happen if I found Philippe. Eric might accuse me of letting him take me there under

false pretenses. As for Philippe, I dreaded his
reaction.

As we entered the little town, with its flat-roofed
houses and modern minarets, I wondered if my
search was really going to end in that isolated spot
at the edge of the Sahara.

Eric parked the car in front of a hotel with freshly
whitewashed walls.

"We'll have lunch here," he said. "Come on."

We went inside. The faded hangings and battered
chairs in the dining room had seen better days, but
the view from the windows was magnificent. The
hotel was built on a high, steep cliff overlooking a
vast, rocky wasteland.

"Are there any other hotels in Yeffren?" I asked
when we had sat down at a table and ordered our
meal.

"Not that I know of. Don't you like this one?"

"Oh yes, it's not that.... If Philippe were in
Yeffren, would he have to stay here?"

"What are you driving at? You're hiding something from me."

I showed him the telegram. He was thoughtful for
a few moments when he'd finished reading it.

"So that's why you had a sudden desire to see the
desert. You could have told me."

"I wanted you to come with me, and I was afraid
you'd refuse if you knew."

"In that case, you're forgiven. The manager of the

hotel speaks French. Maybe he can tell us something."

He called over the waiter and asked to see the manager, who came to our table a minute later.

"We're looking for a friend who's supposed to be staying at your hotel," Eric said to him.

"What's his name?"

"Cottens. Philippe Cottens."

"There's no one here by that name. We don't have many guests now, so I'm sure I'd remember him if he registered here recently."

Although it seemed useless, Eric showed him the telegram. "Ah, yes!" exclaimed the manager. "I called in that message to the telegraph office, only yesterday."

"Who gave it to you?"

"A truck driver who often stops here. He was coming from Sebha. He told me a Frenchman had given him the message and asked him to send it from the telegraph office, but since he was having lunch here, he said it would be more convenient for him if I'd do it by telephone."

"There's no telegraph office in Sebha?" I asked.

"The truck driver had already left Sebha when he was given the message. He was in a village on the way to Yeffren."

"Do you know which village it was?"

"No, he didn't say."

When the manager had left, Eric remarked, "You

have a strange expression, Dina. Is it just disappointment?"

"I *am* disappointed, of course, but something bothers me: why would Philippe have had someone else send the telegram for him?"

"Maybe he's in the middle of the desert and can't get to a town."

"Are you guessing, or do you know something you're not telling me?"

"It's only a supposition. I have no idea what Philippe is doing now, and I don't care. Anyway, he's not here, so as far as you're concerned the day is wasted, isn't it?"

It would have been dishonest of me to answer yes. I admitted I'd enjoyed our drive, and he proposed that we finish it as planned, without giving any more thought to Philippe.

That was easy to say, but after lunch, when we climbed to the top of a tower to view the town, the mountains and the desert, I couldn't help asking, "Eric, do you think I'll ever find Philippe? Sometimes I feel as if I'm chasing a mirage."

"That's because you *are* chasing a mirage, someone who doesn't exist. The honest, boring, faithful man you thought you loved has never existed. The real Philippe is a stranger to you. Why should you be concerned with him?"

"I'm not really looking for Philippe now; I'm looking for answers to the questions that keep running through my mind. Why did he ask me to come to Tripoli? Where is he? Why hasn't he told me what he's doing?"

"What good would it do you to know all that? Things could be so simple, Dina, if you would just forget everything but us!"

"I have to know the truth."

"The truth? I love you; that's the only truth that matters. If you'd only look into your heart, you'd discover what I'm capable of doing for you."

His words went to my head like strong wine, and I didn't try to understand their exact meaning. My will was swept away by the touch of his hand on my arm, and I don't know why I didn't tell him I loved him at that moment. Some secret anxiety prevented me from giving in to that impulse.

"Eric, please give me time to see things more clearly."

"You still need more time?" he asked, deep disappointment in his voice.

"Yes, I'm afraid I do."

We returned to the car, left the town and began driving across the barren landscape. The flatness of the plain was broken only by low, parallel ridges, but the sunlight transformed each grain of sand into a sparkling diamond.

Eric again took up the only subject that interested him.

"We have to take the chance that's been offered to us, Dina. When I heard about your engagement I lost hope for a while, but then I began to realize that I hadn't really lost you yet, because Philippe wasn't worthy of you. I couldn't believe you'd ever marry him. I hoped for an opportunity to be with you once more. When I saw you that night in the Hotel Uaddan, I knew I'd never let anything separate us again. This time I'll do anything to keep you, no matter how great the risk."

"You're being a little melodramatic."

"You can call it what you like, but we're back together and we're going to stay that way. You want to as much as I do. I'm sure of that now, though there have been times when I wondered. When we were in that seaside restaurant, for example, I had the impression that you'd stopped loving me. You ridiculed our past, and like an idiot, I nearly cried."

"Was that the reason? I thought you were thinking of another woman."

"You were jealous? Ah, now I'm sure you love me."

He stopped the car and took me in his arms. We were alone in the vast emptiness of the desert; waves of heat shimmered above the reddish sand. When he kissed me, I didn't struggle against my desire.

He drew back from me with a radiant smile.

"Now you are sure, too," he said emphatically.

"That doesn't prove anything."

"Yes, it does!"

Out of nowhere, a camel appeared behind a thorn bush. To avoid any further admissions, I pointed.

"Look! the desert isn't as deserted as I thought."

But Eric had seen my abandon as proof that he was right, and he was unaffected by my refusal to acknowledge it in words.

AT NIGHTFALL we had to return to civilization. As we passed through a village near Tripoli, a policeman signaled us to stop.

In Italian, he asked Eric for his papers; Eric answered in Arabic. I couldn't follow the conversation, but I gathered that his car registration and driver's license weren't enough, because he searched all his pockets and the glove compartment, then launched into what sounded like an explanation. Finally the policeman nodded and let us go on our way.

"What did he want?"

"My passport, but I don't have it with me. It's lucky he was willing to be reasonable."

Although that day hadn't resolved everything, it had decided one question: I was determined to see Philippe again for the sole purpose of breaking our engagement. I could have simply considered it already broken, of course, but that would have seemed underhanded. I wanted to give him the reasons for my decision and listen to whatever he might want to say in reply. But it was hard for me to imagine anything he could say that would make me change my mind.

Chapter 9

My conscience wouldn't let me go on living at Philippe's expense. The next day I sent my father a telegram asking him to lend me some money and urging him not to tell my mother about it.

As I was leaving the telegraph office I noticed an old Arab on the sidewalk across the street, and nearby, Taoufik. He gave me a friendly smile. I smiled back, but I was beginning to become annoyed by his constant surveillance and decided to escape from him.

I walked through a maze of little side streets till I was sure he'd lost sight of me, then went into a jewelry shop. Soon he scurried past the display window without seeing me. After buying a silver brooch I left the shop, delighted with my clever stratagem. I didn't see Taoufik anywhere, but I did see the old Arab on the sidewalk—the same one who had been in front of the telegraph office. Surely Eric hadn't assigned a second "protector" to me! I decided it must be only a coincidence.

As I was approaching the hotel I glanced over my shoulder. The old Arab had followed me. But he wasn't alone. Taoufik had picked up my trail again, and he waved cheerfully.

When I went into the restaurant Eric was sitting at a table. I immediately attacked him.

"Don't you think you've gone too far?"

"What do you mean?" he asked, instantly on his guard.

"It's bad enough that you've been having me followed by one man, but two!"

"What are you talking about?"

"Don't try to act innocent! This morning Taoufik had a partner: an old Arab who stuck to me like glue."

Eric's face hardened.

"Someone besides Taoufik was following you?"

"As if you didn't know!"

"I didn't. I haven't told anyone else to watch you. You must have imagined it."

"Absolutely not. He was following me; I couldn't possibly have been mistaken."

He seemed worried.

"I don't like this. Excuse me a minute."

He stood up and left me. I couldn't doubt his sincerity. But who else would want to have me followed? I couldn't think of a logical explanation.

Eric came back to the table.

"Dina, you'd better not go out very often for a while. I just talked to Taoufik. You're right: there was someone else."

"Is that what's worrying you?"

"It's not only that. I'm afraid I may have gotten myself into a rather tight spot and I wouldn't like to drag you into it."

"What kind of tight spot?"

"I'm not sure yet. But I want you to be more careful."

"Do you know who was following me?"

"If I did, I wouldn't be so worried."

"Can't you be more specific?"

He shook his head, lost in thought for a few moments.

"I may be making a mountain out of a molehill," he said at last. "Even so, I want you to promise me that you won't slip away from Taoufik again."

"All right, but you can give him the rest of the day off, because I'm staying in the hotel."

As SOON AS I left Eric I had to change my plans. The desk clerk gave me a note that had been left for me during lunch. It was from Marceline Lafont, asking me to come to see her as quickly as possible.

Thinking she must have some news of Philippe, I went to her apartment immediately. She opened the door for me, then bolted it the moment I was inside.

She'd been pale the last time I saw her; now she was white as a sheet, and her eyes were haggard.

I noticed that the photograph of Philippe was no longer in the living room. Before I could question her about it, she said, "I wanted to see you because I have a favor to ask. You must write to Philippe."

"But I don't know where he is!"

She dismissed my objection with a shrug.

"I'm sure you have some way of reaching him. An address in France, his family, one of his friends— anyone who can forward a letter to him."

"What do you want me to write to him about?"

"My passport. He took it from me and I have to get another one. I want him to send me an affidavit saying he took my passport and lost it."

"But why would he have taken it?"

"Well, he. . . . Maybe it was by mistake. Yes, that's it—by mistake."

"What makes you think he lost it?"

"I just think so."

"He didn't tell you he'd lost it?"

"No, but—"

"Then you can't be sure. Maybe he still has it. If so, the simplest thing would be for him to send it back to you."

"No! Don't tell him to do that!" she cried almost hysterically.

She seemed so frantic and irrational that I was beginning to become uneasy about being alone with her.

"I think your problem can easily be solved," I said, trying to sound reassuring, as if I were talking to a fretful child. "All you have to do is go to the French consulate and tell them you lost your passport. They'll give you another one."

"I didn't lose it! Philippe stole it from me!"

"Stole it? But why would he do a thing like that?"

Her expression became suspicious.

"There's no use questioning me. I don't know anything. But I can't go anywhere without a passport. I don't want to go to prison."

I knew nothing about Libyan laws, but it was hard to believe that anyone could be put in prison for not having a passport. Considering her emotional state, however, I thought it best not to argue with her.

"Would you like me to go to the consulate with you?" I asked.

"No. Why won't you write to Philippe?"

"He's not in France. Two days ago he sent me a telegram from Yeffren."

"That's impossible! He left Libya two weeks ago."

"You're mistaken. I checked with a travel agency. He hasn't left the country."

She obviously didn't believe me. She stubbornly repeated that Philippe was in France, that he had stolen her passport and that I had to write to him. To end our conversation, I finally agreed to do it. When finally I left her apartment I breathed a sigh of immense relief.

As I stepped out of the elevator I nearly collided with the old Italian woman.

"You were visiting Marceline?" she asked.

"Yes."

"I hope she's feeling better now."

"Has she been sick?"

"She hasn't left her apartment for the past two weeks, but she won't let me send for a doctor. I've been doing all her shopping for her."

Sickness might explain why Marceline had been staying in her apartment, but I wanted to know how much truth there was in her story about Philippe stealing her passport. I also wanted to know if it was possible, under Libyan law, that she might go to prison for not having one. Eric could tell me that.

When I returned to the hotel I saw that his key wasn't hung up behind the desk, so I assumed he was in his room.

The key had been left in the lock of his door, but when I knocked there was no answer. I knocked again, several times. Still no answer. Finally I opened the door and went in, smiling at the thought that after urgently warning me to be careful, he'd absentmindedly left his key in the lock. His room was open to anyone who might want to come in.

I sat down at the table with the intention of writing a sarcastic note and leaving it in a place where he'd be sure to see it when he came in. I had a pen in my purse, but no paper. Maybe there was some paper in the desk drawer. I tried to open it, but it was stuck. I pulled harder. It yielded so abruptly that I pulled it all the way out and dropped it on the floor, spilling its contents.

I put it back in place, then knelt to pick up the things that had fallen out. It was lucky Eric didn't come in at that moment. What would he have thought if he'd seen me with his letters and business papers scattered in front of me? I was about to put an open envelope back into the drawer when I saw that it contained a passport.

The memory of my conversation with Marceline made me remove the passport and look at it. I started violently when I saw the photograph. I checked the name. The passport was Philippe's.

What was Eric doing with it, and why hadn't he told me about it? I couldn't imagine Philippe giving it to him. They knew each other, but they weren't friends. There must be a plausible explanation.

One thing was certain. Philippe couldn't have left Libya without his passport. And although Eric claimed he didn't know where Philippe was, that was obviously untrue. I couldn't understand why he had lied to me. . . . And then the passport in his drawer . . . .

I recalled the contradictions that had so often puzzled me: Philippe had asked me to come as soon as possible, yet had gone away before I arrived. Then he had insisted that I wait for him, when he must have known that if I stayed in Tripoli I couldn't fail to learn unfavorable things about him.

I realized with a shock that I'd never been in direct contact with him, except for the time when I called him from Paris, and then his voice was almost unrecognizable. Suddenly chilled, I realized that someone else could have sent telegrams in his name, even answered the telephone when I put through my call from Paris.

If so, it must have been someone who had an interest in breaking my engagement to Philippe, someone aware of the damaging rumors about him that were circulating in Tripoli. Someone who was, by his own admission, determined to get me back at any cost.

I remembered Eric saying, "This time I'd do anything to keep you, no matter how great the risk."

Other words and attitudes of his came back into my mind, with different meanings now. He hadn't been surprised to see me in the Hotel Uaddan that first night. He expected me—I was sure of that now. And he'd never been worried that Philippe might come back.

I felt as if I were tottering on the brink of an abyss. My hands were cold and sweaty at the same time. I wished I could stop thinking, but everything fit together too well, the logic implacable.

The reason that Philippe hadn't taken back his passport was that he no longer needed it, that he would never need it again. Eric knew it; he knew

that Philippe wouldn't come back because he was
dead.

I felt on the verge of hysteria. I told myself it must
all be a terrible nightmare. But everything in that
perfectly ordinary hotel room was so real that I
couldn't delude myself.

I stuffed Philippe's passport back into its envelope, hastily piled the other papers into the
drawer and ran away.

After locking myself in my room I lay down on
the bed. For several minutes my mind was blank.
Then the thoughts began returning, and with them
the terrible suspicion that had overwhelmed me. I
desperately struggled against it.

Eric, a murderer? How could I even consider such
a monstrous idea? There had to be some
explanation.

I tried to remember everything that had happened
since the time I received the first telegram. I had no
proof that it had been sent by Philippe. Eric could
easily have sent it. If he had been asked for some
proof of identity, he could have shown Philippe's
passport. The description in it could apply to him,
since they were both tall and dark. The photograph
didn't look like him, of course, but identity
photographs are seldom very good anyway, and this
one was four years old, so the difference could be
attributed to time.

My telephone call from Paris? The voice at the
other end of the line had sounded strange to me. At

the time, I'd assumed it was because of a bad connection; now I realized I couldn't be sure it had been Philippe's voice at all.

The Transtourist Agency had told me that Philippe hadn't come in person to reserve my room or pay my expenses in advance, so it was possible that it was actually Eric who had made the reservation and the payment.

And the telegram that had been sent from Yeffren just when Eric had learned from Taoufik that I was about to go back to France....

I suddenly remembered the note that had been waiting for me when I arrived at the hotel. I took it out to examine it again and realized that while the handwriting in the note itself was unquestionably Philippe's, the address on the envelope was typed. And except for the address, there was no indication that it had even been meant for me. My name wasn't at the top of it. Since it was undated, it could have been written long before, for a completely different purpose.

I gradually became convinced that Eric had sent for me, and that Philippe hadn't even known I was coming.

To carry out such a fraud, Eric had to be certain of not being unmasked, which meant that he knew I'd never see or hear from Philippe again.

Philippe hadn't left Libya; his passport proved that. Yet Marceline Lafont insisted that he hadn't been there for two weeks. But how was it possible to disappear without any trace in a country where the police constantly checked on everyone? The police.... It was Eric who had discouraged me from going to them, by insinuating that I might make trouble for Philippe.

Finally I remembered the thief at Leptis Magna to whom Eric had given money. Had he done it to keep him from talking? And that anxiety he hadn't been able to hide for the past few days....

I tried to reject all this evidence, refusing to accept what seemed to be the answer to the questions tormenting me ever since my arrival in Tripoli. I felt that the truth lay before me, but I didn't want to look at it. Had Eric loved me enough to be capable of murder?

If so, I was partly responsible: I'd refused to listen to him in the past; I'd become engaged to a man I didn't love; and now I was more concerned with protecting Eric than with avenging his victim. I knew I wouldn't have the courage to turn him over to the police even if my assumptions became a certainty, even if he confessed to me....

But I didn't want to hear his confession. The next day, I would take a plane back to France without seeing him again, without reading in his eyes what he had done. I had to leave myself the possibility of doubt.

There was a knock on the door. I sat up, hesitating.

"Dina, it's me, Eric."

From the shudder that ran through me I realized

that in spite of my determination not to pass final judgment I believed he was guilty, since the sound of his voice was enough to fill me with horror.

Fifteen minutes later the telephone rang. I didn't answer it. It rang a long time before silence returned. I continued lying on my bed, fully dressed, unable to shed the tears I felt rising. I turned off the light and eventually drifted into a tortured sleep.

When I awoke, it was daylight. It took me several seconds to remember what had happened. My anguish returned in a rush, but sleep had given me some strength to resist it. The night before, I'd let myself be carried away by my imagination; I'd accused Eric on the basis of fragile deductions. If I examined things calmly, I'd laugh at the absurd theory I'd concocted.

But again, the more I thought about it, the more convinced I became that it was Eric who had made me come to Tripoli, and I was faced with the same questions. How had he known Philippe wouldn't come back? Only he could have told me, but that morning I still didn't have the courage to talk to him. I was afraid he'd lie, and worse, lie badly. There was no choice: I had to leave. If I stayed, I wouldn't be able to keep quiet very long. How I regretted having canceled my plane reservation to France!

I changed from my rumpled clothes and called the Transtourist Agency. They promised to get me a reservation as soon as possible but said it would be difficult because many Libyan engineers and technicians were going to a convention in Rome, so the planes were all booked for the next few days. If there was a cancellation, I would be notified immediately.

To avoid meeting Eric, I left the hotel before lunchtime and ate in a little restaurant where the food was too rich in olive oil for my taste. Then I spent more than an hour walking aimlessly, trying to distract myself from the disturbing thoughts that refused to leave my mind.

Chapter 10

When I returned to the hotel I went up to my room and stopped in the doorway, frozen in surprise. Eric was sitting in my armchair.

He stood up. "What kind of game are you playing? Yesterday you locked yourself in and wouldn't answer the phone, and today you didn't come to the hotel restaurant for lunch."

I looked at him as if he was an enemy. To give myself time to control the nervous trembling that had come over me, I slowly walked into the room and closed the door behind me before asking, "How did you get here?"

My voice sounded unnatural. He misinterpreted my emotion.

"I bribed a maid to unlock your door. Does that shock you?"

I shook my head.

He stepped toward me and I instinctively moved back.

"What's the matter, Dina? You act as if you're afraid of me."

I *was* afraid, but not for myself. I glanced at the door, longing to escape. He grasped me by the wrists and said, "Tell me what's wrong."

And I knew I had to tell him. I couldn't turn back now.

"Yesterday you left the key in the lock of your door. I went into your room. . . . "

My voice failed me. He obviously had no idea of what I was about to say, because he asked impatiently, "Well? What was so strange about my room?"

"I didn't mean to be indiscreet. I only wanted to write you a note. I opened your drawer to look for some paper . . . and I found Philippe's passport."

He reacted in the way I least expected: he laughed.

"And that's why you're so upset?"

"Yes, I. . . . That passport. . . . Oh, Eric, what have you done?"

"Nothing to justify the look of tragedy on your face. It's not a crime."

The casual way he said this should have enlightened me, but I was in no condition to think clearly. I could only repeat, "Not a crime . . . not a crime. . . . Oh, my God!"

"What's come over you?"

He released my wrists, took me by the shoulders and said harshly, "Look me in the eyes! You don't actually think I...."

He paused, waiting for me to give him some indication that he'd misjudged me, that I hadn't really dreamed up such an idea. I was unable to say anything. He took my silence as an admission and turned livid with rage.

"You're insane!" he shouted. "You think I'm a murderer, don't you? Yes, you do, I can see it in your eyes! Why don't you say it? Go on, say it!"

All at once he pushed me away, sat down again and covered his face with his hands. His anger was a sign of innocence, but I'd been too strongly in the grip of my nightmare to be reassured so easily.

"Eric, why do you have that passport?"

He remained motionless, as if nothing mattered any more. I wasn't even sure he had heard me.

"Answer me, Eric."

"What's the use?" he murmured bitterly.

"You must tell me the truth. You lied to me, didn't you? You know where Philippe is."

He looked up at me.

"Yes, I lied to you, even more than you think, but I don't know where Philippe is. You want me to tell you the truth? I will, but it's not important now. I loved you, Dina. And you thought.... You've known me for years, but that didn't stop you from accusing me of murder!"

He stood up again and began pacing the floor. I

couldn't accept his reproaches when he'd just admitted his deceit.

"What else could I think? I finally realized that Philippe hadn't asked me to come here. You sent those telegrams and had someone else answer the phone when I tried to call Philippe from Paris, didn't you?"

"Yes, I did. It was a big gamble, but I was ready to risk anything for you."

"How could you be sure Philippe wouldn't come back? How did you get his passport? If I assumed the worst, it was because I couldn't see any other explanation."

"So you thought I'd killed Philippe. To you, that was a plausible explanation."

"I didn't really believe it, I tried not to."

"It's too late to protest, now that I know what was in your mind. There's really no point in saying anything more but, since you want to know, I'll tell you how I got Philippe's passport: he gave it to me, in exchange for mine. Why? I'm not sure any more.

"I began seeing him as soon as I came to Libya. I was surprised at how friendly he was. He often invited me to dinner and seemed eager for us to be on good terms. I never told him that you and I had once been engaged though I think he may have known. He constantly talked about you to me. I knew about the other women in his life: Marceline Lafont and Abed's sister. It infuriated me that I couldn't tell you, but I knew you'd never forgive me if I did, because you'd think I was doing it out of spite. So I tried to think of some other way to prevent your stupid marriage.

"One day Philippe came to me and asked me to help him. While he was driving through a village, he said, he'd accidentally run down a man on the road. He didn't stop because he knew there was a risk that the villagers would lynch him, but instead of going to the nearest police station, reporting the accident and asking for protection, as he should have done, he lost his head and continued on his way to Tripoli. He soon found out that the man had died and that several people had seen his license number as he was driving away.

"He wanted to leave Libya before he was arrested, tried for manslaughter and sent to prison. But the police were already looking for him. If he went to the airport, he'd be arrested before he could get on a plane ... unless he was traveling under a different name. So he wanted me to lend him my passport, since our physical descriptions were similar."

"What about the photograph?" I asked.

"With patience and skill, a specialist can take the photograph out of a passport, put in another one and imitate the original stamp. It's easier to alter a real passport than to make a false one, and it's also quicker. Philippe claimed there was no risk. I knew that wasn't true, but I agreed to do it anyway."

"Why?"

"Because I immediately realized how I could take

advantage of the situation. This was the chance I'd been waiting for and I wasn't going to let it slip away."

"Philippe didn't know your motives. What made him think you'd be willing to do him such a big favor?"

"He had an argument that he considered irresistible: he offered me money, a huge amount. That should have put me on my guard."

"And did he pay you?"

"The fact that you've even asked that question shows your opinion of me. No, he didn't pay me. I refused to take his money. I said I'd help him out of friendship."

"Did he believe you?"

"He needed my passport too much to worry about my motives. I made a plane reservation in my name and picked up the ticket myself. By the time we exchanged passports, I'd worked out my plan. I had him write the note you found waiting for you when you first came to the Hotel Uaddan."

"What reason did you give him for wanting it?"

"I said it would help me to cover myself if anyone asked me where he was. I also made him promise not to see or write to anyone in France before I got my passport back. He was supposed to send it to me as soon as he'd had my photograph reinserted, and I was supposed to send his passport to him as soon as he gave me an address. I haven't heard from him since."

"Since he presumably doesn't need your passport any more, why hasn't he sent it to you?"

"I wish I knew, though I'm beginning to get an idea. At first I was so anxious to see you again and so afraid my scheme might fail that nothing else mattered. I wanted you to come to Tripoli and discover for yourself what kind of man Philippe was. I was afraid he'd go straight to you in Paris and marry you. When you came here—"

I didn't let him go on.

"You lied to me from the start. Everything was false: the telegrams, the phone call, what you told me. . . . I never would have thought you could be so deceitful."

He laughed sarcastically.

"Why not? Since you thought I was a murderer, it shouldn't have been hard for you to believe I was also a liar."

I struggled to understand all that had happened, now that I finally knew the truth. I'd thought I was involved in a tragedy, but it had turned out to be only a farce, performed at my expense.

"Who answered when I called from Paris?"

"Taoufik. I needed a partner."

"You mean an accomplice. Why did you have him follow me?"

"I wanted him to guard you and keep me posted on what you were doing. I knew you'd try to find Philippe. He has some unsavory friends in Tripoli, and I was worried about what might happen if you made contact with them."

"What about that man at Leptis Magna? Why did you give him money?"

"Most of what I told you about him was true, but I omitted a few things. He had a temporary job at the airport on the day when Philippe left. He recognized him from having seen him at the Hotel Uaddan and saw him get into a plane. I didn't want you to know that, of course, so I gave him some money and promised not to have him arrested if he kept quiet."

"You didn't think you could keep up your deception forever, did you?"

"No, sooner or later I'd have told you everything."

"What were you waiting for?"

"I was waiting for you to realize you loved me. I couldn't be absolutely sure unless you told me so yourself, directly and without reserve. Then I'd have told you everything. I hoped you'd forgive me when you knew my reasons."

But I couldn't forgive him for the hours of anguish I'd just been through, any more than he could forgive me for having suspected him of murder.

"And why was that old Arab following me yesterday?"

"I don't know."

"That's what you said yesterday. Were you telling the truth, for once?"

"Yes, I was."

"Then—"

"There are still some things I haven't told you. I wanted to use Philippe as a means of getting you back and I thought he believed my lie about helping him out of friendship. But I later found out that *he* was using *me* and that he'd been as dishonest with me as I'd been with him. I became suspicious when I noticed nothing in the newspapers about the accident he claimed to have had. I checked with the police and learned that there hadn't been any such accident."

"You think he invented it? Then what was his real reason for wanting to leave the country?"

"At first I thought he was afraid of being prosecuted by the E.R.P.C., but I checked with them, too: they have no intention of prosecuting him, and he knew that when he left the company.

"A few days ago, Taoufik told me something that suggested another explanation. He'd discovered that Saad Abed's sister, Meryem, had run away from home. The family managed to hush it up for a while, but gradually the story leaked out. With the help of a maid who was devoted to her, Meryem had been secretly meeting a European man. Her brother found out about it and ordered her to stop. She seemed willing to obey him, but then one morning she went shopping with her maid and neither of them came back.

"It's rumored that she went to a friend's house and came out wearing European clothes, with her hair dyed red. Since she'd always worn a veil except when she was at home, not many people had ever seen her face, so there wasn't much danger of her being recognized in public. Someone, probably Philippe, helped her to leave Tripoli. As for the maid, she went back to her nomadic tribe in the Fezzan region and hasn't been seen since."

"Why do you think it was probably Philippe who helped Meryem to leave?"

"Partly because his affair with her was well known, and mainly because she disappeared on the day he left. I'm afraid Abed may have reached the same conclusion, and that he's the one who's begun having you followed."

I remembered my conversation with Abed and the veiled animosity he had shown toward Philippe.

"Even if Philippe did take Meryem away, I don't see why he'd need a false identity. Why couldn't he have traveled under his own name?"

"First of all, she's only seventeen, so he could be charged with abducting a minor, even if she said she was willing to go with him. Then there's Abed. If Philippe had made a plane reservation in his own name, Abed probably would have found out about it. He would have dealt with the matter personally, without calling in the police, and that would have been even worse, because he's a cruel and powerful man."

"If you'd known what Philippe intended to do, would you have refused to lend him your passport?"

Eric hesitated but finally admitted, "No. Nothing could have made me give up that chance of seeing you again."

"What are you risking? Prison?"

"If there was a trial, it would be hard for me to prove I hadn't been Philippe's accomplice. But there won't be a trial. Abed wouldn't want his sister's dishonor to be made public."

"Where do you suppose she is now?"

"I have no idea. I assume she's with Philippe, but they could be anywhere. She must be traveling with a false passport too."

Yes, of course. I suddenly realized how Philippe had secured her a passport. But I didn't tell Eric.

"Any more questions?" he asked.

"No."

"Well, now that you know all the answers, you can go back to France. If you want me to, I'll make a reservation for you."

The coldness of his tone didn't hide his unhappiness, but my resentment against him was so strong that I couldn't feel sorry for him. What had he hoped to achieve by his elaborate machinations? Had he really believed our love could be revived with lies and trickery?

"Never mind, I'll do it myself. And it goes without saying that I'll reimburse you for all the money you've spent on me."

He stepped back as if I'd slapped him, then said curtly, "If you feel it's necessary."

When Eric left my room I looked at my watch. I still had time to go to the Transtourist Agency. I wanted to make a reservation as soon as possible, and I also wanted to find out if I was right about something.

At the agency, I went to the same clerk I'd talked with before.

"You're in luck," she said to me. "There's just been a cancellation. I can give you a reservation for the day after tomorrow."

I took it. Then I asked her if she still had the passenger lists she'd checked when I'd wanted to know if Philippe had left the country. She showed them to me and I quickly found what I was looking for. On the day when I received the first telegram signed "Philippe," a passenger by the name of Eric Darnal had taken a plane to Rome, and a few hours later a passenger named Marceline Lafont had taken a plane to Paris, via Rome.

Poor Marceline! She was the only one I pitied. She was afraid of going to prison, but she'd done nothing wrong. Philippe had stolen her passport and abandoned her to her fate.

I left the agency and went to her apartment only to find her more terrified than ever. When I told her I now knew why Philippe had stolen her passport, she informed me that he'd just sent it back to her, without a word of explanation or apology.

"Then you have nothing to worry about," I said.

"No, you don't understand! Philippe used my

passport to get Abed's sister out of the country, and it was stamped with the date she left. If the police had seen it, it would have been enough to convict me as an accomplice to the abduction of a minor. I burned it to keep it from being used as evidence against me. But I'm still afraid. If only I could go back to France and feel safe again, without having to wonder every night if—"

"You don't have to be afraid any more. There won't be a trial, so you can't be convicted."

"There are worse things than going to prison. You don't know what kind of a man Abed is! He feels his honor has been offended by what happened to his sister, and he'll try to get revenge on everyone involved."

"But you weren't involved. Your passport was stolen."

"He doesn't know that. He'll think I gave it to Philippe. Besides, he's angry about more than his honor. His sister was about to marry an influential man who would have been very helpful to him as a brother-in-law. Now, of course, there's no chance that the marriage will ever take place. I hate to think of how furious Abed must be."

"What makes you think he knows his sister used your passport?"

"He knows. One of his men is in front of this building now, waiting for me to come out."

I tried to convince her she was mistaken, that her fear was making her imagine things. I didn't succeed but she finally relaxed a little and began talking about Philippe. When she had come to Tripoli, after having known him before, in France, he had told her that his engagement to me was a foolish mistake that he'd already corrected. He'd introduced her everywhere as his future wife, but she soon realized that he was using her as a way of diverting suspicion from himself and Meryem.

"Did you tell Philippe you knew what he was doing?" I asked.

"Yes, and of course he denied it. He said he had a big sum of money at stake in his business arrangements with Abed and that he wasn't stupid enough to risk losing it by flirting with Meryem. He and Abed were involved in something to do with oil concessions. I don't know much about it, except that they'd already made a lot of money from it and were expecting to make even more. And then Philippe ran away with Meryem. I never would have thought he'd give up all that money just to be with her!"

"Why didn't he wait till he had it before going off with her?"

"She was about to be married, so he couldn't wait any longer."

I couldn't help thinking that Philippe at least deserved credit for putting love about money, but I kept that thought to myself. Marceline wouldn't have appreciated my indulgence.

I told her I'd do anything I could to help her, though I didn't have the heart to tell her I was leaving in two days.

Chapter 11

Since my remaining time in Tripoli would probably be too short to allow me to help Marceline effectively, I decided to ask Eric to do something, but that evening he didn't come to the hotel restaurant for dinner. I was afraid he would see a phone call as an attempt at reconciliation, so I decided to wait till the next day to ask him.

But the next day brought a great surprise: a letter from Philippe, forwarded by my mother. I was amazed to see that it bore a Libyan stamp and had been postmarked at Youffra four days earlier. With it came a note from my mother, who had thought we were together, asking me why Philippe had written to me in Paris. To me, the question was why his letter had been mailed in Libya when I thought he was in France.

What he wrote answered very little. Expressing

deep regret and making elaborate efforts to be tactful, he told me that after long, careful consideration he had reached the conclusion that it would be a mistake for us to be married. In short, he broke our engagement.

I had to see Eric, so I called him, no longer caring how he might interpret it. After he promised to meet me for lunch, I spent the rest of the morning imagining all sorts of farfetched explanations and rejecting them one after another.

In the restaurant, Eric treated me even more distantly than he had done the day before. He greeted me stiffly and asked why I wanted to see him. I told him about Philippe's letter, and he showed no surprise.

"He's not only in Libya, he's also in Tripoli," he said. "He called me just after you did and I went to see him. I gave him back his passport and he gave me mine, with my photograph in it, showing no sign of ever having been removed. The job was done by an expert."

"He came back after abducting a minor? You told me that was a crime."

"It is, but there's no proof that he committed it."

"Yesterday you thought—"

"I must have been mistaken. I'm sure he wouldn't have come back, even to get a large sum of money, if he'd thought he was in any danger from Abed. He knows how Abed deals with his enemies."

"Did he give you any explanation?"

"He said he no longer had to worry about his accident because the charges against him had been dropped; he'd come back to settle a business matter."

"Did you talk to him about Meryem?"

"Of course. He claimed he didn't know she'd run away from home; she wasn't on his plane and if she left on the same day he did, it was only a coincidence."

"Do you believe that?"

He shrugged.

"I don't care enough about it to decide whether I believe it or not."

'He lied to you. Meryem did leave on the same day he did and it was no coincidence. He'd given her Marceline's passport."

A glimmer of interest appeared in Eric's eyes.

"How do you know?"

I told him what I'd learned from Marceline and the Transtourist Agency.

"I knew Philippe was unscrupulous," he remarked, "but I didn't know he was so reckless. If Abed has the slightest suspicion...."

"Eric, can you help Marceline?"

"Why me? Why not ask Philippe?"

"I don't want to see him."

"I think you'll have to whether you like it or not, because he's staying in this hotel."

"Did you tell him I was here?"

"No."

"Then maybe I can avoid him till tomorrow morning. I'm leaving then."

Eric's face remained expressionless. After having said and done so much to prove his love to me, he now seemed totally detached.

"That will be better for both of us," he said.

It was an admission of failure. His attempts to revive the past had driven us farther apart than ever.

THAT AFTERNOON I packed my suitcases. Soon I would be back in Paris, trying to forget my stay in Tripoli. I'd already said goodbye to Eric: he'd told me that he wouldn't take me to the airport the next day and wouldn't be in the hotel when I left. He hadn't explained why he would be gone and I'd felt it would be pointless to ask.

It would take me a long time to resign myself to our separation, but when I remembered his lies I was sure that nothing was possible between us. His conduct seemed all the more unforgivable to me because he hadn't expressed any remorse. He acted as if his feelings justified the means he had used, as if only I was in the wrong, because I'd suspected him of murder. That hardened my resentment and I had no inclination to find excuses for him.

As for Philippe, I hadn't the slightest desire to see him again. I could have asked him about certain things that were still obscure, but there was no reason to believe he'd be more honest with me than he'd been with Eric. And I had no interest in knowing his plans for the future; they no longer concerned me.

At twilight, feeling that I had to get out of my room for a while, I took a walk to the waterfront. The sea, smooth as a lake, was reddened by the setting sun.

I waited till darkness had fallen before returning to the hotel. A policeman was waiting for me in the lobby. I couldn't help feeling apprehensive as he approached me, even though I knew I hadn't done anything illegal.

He told me in Italian that I was needed for an identification. An injured man, apparently the victim of a hit-and-run driver, had been found on a road twenty miles outside of Tripoli and taken to a hospital. He had no papers except an envelope with my name and address at the Hotel Uaddan typed on it, containing a photograph.

The policeman showed it to me. It was a picture of me that I'd given Philippe a year earlier. The only explanation I could think of was that he'd somehow learned I was at the Uaddan and decided to send it back to me there, maybe with a note that he hadn't had time to write.

I said I was sure the man was Philippe Cottens and asked how badly he was hurt. The policeman hesitated a moment before answering.

"I'm afraid he's in very serious condition. Will you come to the hospital to identify him?"

"Yes."

As I rode through the city in a police car, I felt only pity for Philippe. Although I couldn't excuse what he had done, it seemed obvious that he wouldn't have run such a great risk if he hadn't been deeply in love with Meryem. But why hadn't he stayed in France with her? He must have realized the danger of returning to Libya and exposing himself to Abed's vengeance. I wondered, of course, if his injury had been accidental, or if Abed was behind it. How tragic, I thought, if after having tried so hard to find him I was going to see him again just as he was about to die.

In the hospital, the policeman led me along a hall, stopped in front of a door, opened it and stepped aside to let me enter.

At first I saw only a nurse standing beside the bed, but when I drew nearer, I had to stifle a scream.

The deathly pale man lying unconscious on the bed was Eric.

"Is that Philippe Cottens?" the policeman asked quietly.

I shook my head, suddenly realizing that everything that had turned us against each other had ceased to matter.

I leaned down, kissed Eric on the lips and whispered, "I'll never leave you again. Never."

The nurse told me I couldn't stay any longer. I walked out of the room with the policeman following. In the hall, he ordered me politely but firmly to come with him.

Hardly knowing what I was doing, I walked beside him along a corridor till we came to an office, where he asked me to sit down. He left and came back a few minutes later with another policeman. They both began questioning me insistently. What was the injured man's name? What was he doing in Libya? When was the last time I'd seen him? Had he told me what he intended to do that day? Why had I thought at first that he was Philippe Cottens?

I answered conscientiously, wanting to escape from them as soon as I could, but they tirelessly continued their interrogation. Finally I lost patience and begged them to let me go back to Eric. They told me the doctors had given orders that he wasn't to have any visitors. I asked to speak with the doctors; they said it was impossible.

At last, when they became convinced that I'd really told them everything I knew, they let me go.

As I was leaving the office I saw Taoufik.

"Oh, Taoufik, I'm so glad you're here! You know about Eric?"

"Yes. Have you seen him?"

"Only for a few seconds, and they won't let me go back. They won't even let me talk to the doctors. I have to know if he's—"

"Let's not stay here."

He saw a nurse coming toward us, stopped her

and said a few words to her in Arabic. She took us to a room where we could be alone.

"You must be calm," said Taoufik, seeing my haggard expression. "Eric's condition is serious but not hopeless."

"Who told you so?"

"One of the doctors." He lowered his voice. "Don't ask too many questions. They won't let you come back to the hospital if they think you don't accept their version of what happened to Eric."

"What do you mean?"

"He wasn't in an accident. Someone tried to kill him. He was stabbed."

"Stabbed!"

"Officially, there are no clues. If you want my personal opinion, Saad Abed ordered it done."

"Abed? Eric hasn't done anything to him."

"No, but he was indirectly involved in Meryem's leaving the country."

"Because he lent Philippe his passport? But Philippe is back in Tripoli now. Why wouldn't Abed have tried to kill him, instead of Eric?"

"I don't know, and I can't even try to guess."

"How did you find out Eric had been stabbed?"

"From a friend of mine in the police force. He also told me Eric was found on the road to Yeffren, but of course that doesn't necessarily mean he was stabbed there. His attackers may have taken him out of the city and left him on the road, thinking he was dead. The police have said he was apparently hit by a car, and that's one reason why I think Abed ordered him stabbed. He's a very powerful man. You mustn't say anything to contradict the official version."

I told him that as far as I was concerned, the police could say whatever they liked; all I wanted was to see Eric again. He promised to do his best to get visiting privileges for me, though he wasn't sure he'd succeed. In a hospital, it was always easy to use medical reasons as a pretext for isolating a patient.

I told him about the photograph. He'd already seen it: Philippe had inadvertently left it in his passport, and Eric had kept it. But why had he put it in an envelope addressed to me?

My absurd quarrel with Eric now seemed so remote that it was hard for me to understand how I could have felt the way I did. I'd refused to forgive him for the scheme that had brought me to Tripoli; yet he'd done it only because he loved me and could see no other way of making me realize I still loved him. And he was right: I'd never stopped loving him. If only I'd been honest enough to admit it from the start.

What would I have done without Taoufik? His friendship gradually helped me regain my courage. When he told me that his friend in the police force would keep him constantly posted on Eric's condition, I gave in to his insistence that I return to the hotel.

But when I was alone in my room, my newfound courage abandoned me. I began sobbing, sick with anxiety. Then a terrifying thought occurred to me : if Taoufik was right and it was Abed who had tried to have Eric killed, he would soon learn that he'd failed, and there was nothing to prevent him from trying again. Even if Eric recovered, he wouldn't be safe as long as he was in Libya.

The need to cope with that new danger gave me back my self-control. I knew what I had to do.

I got up from my bed, splashed cold water on my face, went downstairs and asked the desk clerk to tell Philippe Cottens, if he was in the hotel, that a friend of Saad Abed was waiting for him in the bar. The clerk made the call in front of me, hung up and informed me that Signor Cottens would be down in a few moments.

I sat down at a vacant table. It was dinnertime, so the bar was nearly empty.

Philippe saw me as soon as he came in. He stared at me as if he couldn't believe his eyes. Since he hadn't known I was in Tripoli he was completely bewildered by my presence.

"You !" he exclaimed incredulously.

He seemed to have changed, probably because I was examining him with different eyes. Before, his ordinary-looking face had inspired confidence in me ; now it gave me an impression of weakness and insincerity. How could I have ever considered spending the rest of my life with this man ? I must have been desperate to wipe away the memory of

Eric, since I'd chosen a man who was his exact
opposite!

"Sit down," I said calmly. "I'm the one who asked
you to come to the bar."

"But I was told it was a friend of. . . ."

He seemed reluctant to say the name, so I said it
for him.

"Saad Abed. That's right."

"You know him?"

"We'll discuss that later."

He nervously sat down across the table from me.

"But what are you doing in Tripoli, Geraldine?"

"I wanted to see you."

It was perfectly true, but circumstances had made
my answer ironic. If I hadn't been trying to protect
Eric, I would have had no desire to see him.

"Why? And why didn't you tell me you were
coming? It doesn't make sense!"

I had no intention of telling him what Eric had
done. Now that he had become a stranger to me it
didn't concern him.

"You're right, it doesn't make sense."

"How long have you been here?"

"Several days."

He suddenly became very uneasy.

"Did you get my letter?"

"Yes. Don't worry, I couldn't agree with you
more: it would have been a mistake for us to get
married."

"I'm relieved to hear that. But since you received

my letter and you agree with what I said in it, I'm more puzzled than ever. Why are you here?"

"What about you, Philippe? Why have you come back to Tripoli? Where's Meryem?"

He couldn't help looking startled but he quickly recovered his composure.

"You've already heard that gossip? I hardly knew her and I had nothing to do with her disappearance. I didn't find out about it till I came back, and then I heard the rumors that I was responsible for it! It's ridiculous!"

"She didn't take the same plane as you, but she left on the same day."

His face took on an amazed expression.

"What are you talking about? What plane?"

"A plane to Rome."

"You think I went to Rome? I never left Libya! I went to the southern part of the country and spent two weeks with a Berber friend of mine in an isolated oasis. I'd begun to feel that you and I should break our engagement but I didn't want to make such an important decision lightly, so I went to a place where I could think things out."

I ignored his explanation and asked skeptically, "You were in Libya the whole time?"

"I haven't left the country in six months. I'll prove it to you, since you seem to doubt it. Here, you can see for yourself." He took out his passport and handed it to me. "Look at the dates stamped in it. If I'd crossed the border, there would be a record of it in my passport. As I've already told you, I was in the southern part of the country."

I had no need to examine a passport that had been in Eric's drawer while Philippe was gone. But I still didn't know why he hadn't been afraid to come back and face Abed's anger.

"Is that what you told Abed ?"

"You still haven't told me if you know him."

"Never mind that now. Answer my question : did you tell Abed you'd been in the south, and did he believe you ?"

"Yes, and of course he believed me. If I'd taken a plane, my name would have been on the passenger list."

"Did you suggest that he check the passenger list to make sure you were telling the truth ?"

"He doesn't need any suggestions from me."

"But you didn't tell him you'd borrowed Eric's passport on a false pretext and traveled under his name, did you ?"

He pretended to be perplexed.

"Eric ? Eric Darnal ? What does he have to do with all this ?"

"You didn't take a plane to Rome with Eric's passport ? You didn't give it back to him yesterday ?"

"Absolutely not ! Where did you ever get such an idea ? If Eric claims I borrowed his passport, he's out of his mind !"

If I hadn't had proof that he was lying, I'd have been impressed by his righteous anger.

"You deny it?"

"I give you my word it's not true!"

"Between your word and Eric's, it's easy for me to choose."

In spite of my determination to remain calm, my anxiety about Eric made my voice falter. Philippe notice my emotion and drew a conclusion from it that seemed to delight him.

"Ah, yes, I was forgetting: Eric was your first love."

"My first and only love. I don't wish you any harm, Philippe, but because of you, Eric may be dying...."

"Why? Is he sick? If so, how is it my fault?"

"He was stabbed today. Because you used his passport."

Philippe turned pale.

"Who did it?"

I told him what I knew about the attempt to kill Eric.

"There's no proof that Abed was behind it," he said, "and even if he was, I had nothing to do with it. I never used Eric's passport."

"On the day when you left Tripoli, someone took a plane to Rome under Eric's name. I saw the passenger list."

"What's the matter with you, Geraldine? You're making up complicated explanations for something very simple. If someone took a plane with Eric's passport, it was Eric himself."

"He never left Libya."

"Someone who travels around as much as he does can easily go away for a few days without anyone noticing it. But it's easy to find out if he left the country or not. All you have to do is look at his passport."

Everything suddenly became clear to me and I realized how carefully Philippe had prepared his alibi. His absence must have been shorter than I'd thought. He'd been gone only long enough to place Meryem in the care of someone he could trust. He didn't want to travel on the same plane with her but he had to meet her when she arrived : since she was only seventeen and had had such a secluded upbringing, she wouldn't have possessed the courage to plunge into such an adventure if she hadn't known he would be there to guide her. So he had left a few hours before she did and waited for her at the Rome airport. Then he had come back to Libya and probably spent some time in the southern part of the country so that he could back up his story if necessary.

He had used Eric not only as a means of taking Meryem away, but also as a guarantee that he could shield himself from the consequences of his act. Was he the one who had turned Abed's suspicion toward Eric ? Had he planned from the start to make Eric his scapegoat ?

"Can you explain why Meryem traveled with Marceline Lafont's passport?" I asked.

"You really are well informed! Who told you about Marceline?"

"I know her."

"And Meryem had her passport? I didn't know that."

"You're not going to claim that Marceline gave it to her, are you?"

"No, I'm sure she didn't give it to her. But Marceline is always short of money, so—"

"It's unlucky for you, Philippe, that I'm able to ruin the beautiful plan you've put together. Everything you've told me is false and I can prove it."

"I've had enough of this! Your accusations are insulting and ridiculous! I've been patient till now, but I'm not going to waste any more time listening to such nonsense."

He made a move to stand up.

"Stay here!" I ordered.

Something in my tone must have made him decide it would be better not to defy me.

"All right, I'll listen," he said resignedly, "but make it short."

"You've asked me if I know Abed. I do. I've been here longer than you think. I've had time to meet many people and learn many things. I know about your affairs with Marceline and Meryem, and why you were fired from the E.R.P.C. You stole Marce-

line's passport and gave it to Meryem. She'll testify
to that if necessary.''

"Marceline ? Who would believe her ? What good
is the testimony of a woman who's been abandoned
by her lover and accuses him of theft, out of spite ?''

"I can add my testimony to hers. You gave Eric
your passport in exchange for his. I saw it myself.''

For the first time, he seemed seriously alarmed.

"You have a lot of imagination, but no one will
believe you either. You're trying to show that Eric is
innocent. The police are used to false witnesses.''

"I won't go to the police ; I'll go to Abed, and he'll
believe me, especially since I'm not the only one who
knows the truth. A friend of Eric's has known about
everything from the beginning. Furthermore, a man
who knew you from having worked at the Hotel
Uaddan was at the airport on the day you left, and
he saw you board the plane.''

Philippe's face sagged and he was silent for a few
moments.

"What can I say ? Appearances are against me.''

"Not appearances, facts. Why go on denying
everything ? You know very well that Abed will
believe what I tell him.''

"Abed ! Why do you keep harping back to him ?
He had nothing to do with Eric's stabbing—he's too
cautious to take a risk like that.''

"If you believe that, why did you lie to me ?''

He was about to protest ; then he suddenly
decided to change his tactics.

"Because he owes me money—a lot of money. You're right: Meryem left because of me, and I borrowed Eric's passport. But I didn't think I was putting him in any danger. I still don't think so. Abed wouldn't use such methods, but he's perfectly capable of refusing to pay me what he owes me."

"So it's not enough for you to have Meryem?"

My sarcasm didn't affect him.

"Meryem and I love each other. Abed would never have let me marry her if she'd stayed here, so I arranged for her to leave. He doesn't know that. If he did, he'd get even with me by keeping money that's rightfully mine."

"Aren't you afraid he'd get even with you in a more drastic way? Hasn't anyone ever told you that he's completely ruthless and powerful enough to kill his enemies without having to worry about being brought to trial for it?"

"That's nothing but rumor!"

"I don't think it's rumor, and I want him to stop believing Eric is guilty. If you don't tell him the truth, I will."

"Why? Even if he actually is the one who had Eric stabbed, it won't do Eric any good if Abed goes after me."

"It will keep him from making another attempt to have Eric killed. The next one might be successful."

"You don't really believe that. What you want is revenge against me."

"I'm afraid you're not that important to me. I

don't care what happens to you. Nothing matters to me but Eric."

"Eric was always the only one who mattered to you, wasn't he? You're accusing me, Geraldine, but do you have any right to judge me? Do you think you're completely in the right?"

"Neither of us is completely in the right. I'm not interested in discussing which of us has more cause for complaint, but with others your conduct was inexcusable. Marceline, for example—"

"Marceline! You're not going to say I was wrong to walk out on her, are you? I didn't love her; she was chasing me and at first I didn't have the strength to refuse to see her. My engagement with you was a fraud, since you still loved Eric, so when Marceline offered me her devotion I took it. Then, when I met Meryem, I knew I couldn't go on being satisfied with Marceline just because she wanted me. Marceline is dull, coarse and not even pretty. Meryem is beautiful and charming, and she loves me with all her heart. She's given me everything, but she was about to be married to a man her brother had chosen. He'd never have let her break her engagement and marry me. We had no choice. You ought to understand, instead of condemning me."

"I might have understood if you hadn't been willing to sacrifice Eric and Marceline to get what you wanted. As it is, I have no choice, either."

He must have sensed my determination and

realized it would be futile to try to make me change my mind.

"I can't stop you from going to Abed, but at least give me time to ... settle my business affairs. A few days."

"I'll only give you time to save your life by leaving Libya, provided you write a letter to Abed telling him everything, including the fact that Eric and Marceline were your victims and not your accomplices. If you write that letter and give it to me, I'll wait until you're gone before I send it to Abed."

"And when do you want me to leave?"

"Tomorrow."

"What! I can't leave that soon! I won't be able to get a seat on a plane—"

"You'll have a seat on a flight to Rome at eleven tomorrow morning. It's already reserved in my name. The agency will have time to transfer it to you. I'll give you my ticket."

"Please give me a few more days, Geraldine," he begged. "It's very important."

If I hadn't been so unhappy, I would have laughed at his brazen indecency in asking for a delay in order to collect his profit from the vicious scheme that had left Eric lying on a hospital bed, hovering between life and death.

"I've given you till eleven tomorrow morning and not one minute more. You'll just have to kiss your money goodbye!"

HALF AN HOUR later Philippe handed me the letter. I read it. The explanations in it told me nothing I hadn't already known, though I was surprised by a passage in which he described his love for Meryem in lyrical terms and pleaded with Abed to let them be married immediately. Abed's permission was necessary because she was still a minor and he was her legal guardian. Another passage made me smile: Philippe said he was giving up all claim to the money Abed owned him in order to prove the sincerity of his feelings!

I dropped the letter into my purse and gave him my plane ticket. He left without a word. We had nothing more to say to each other.

Chapter 12

The days that followed were filled with terrible anxiety for me.

Eric's condition was still precarious. Debilitated by pain, fever and medication, he didn't even have the strength to speak, but he was able to smile faintly at me, and those smiles kept me from losing hope.

I spent most of each day in the hospital and visited him often, because as soon as I sent Philippe's confession to Abed, the order forbidding me to see Eric had been withdrawn, as though by a wave of a magic wand. And from then on Eric was treated as a very special patient. The doctors and nurses spared no effort to give him the best possible care. I even learned that Abed personally called every day to ask about him.

The police had questioned me again. I'd been

careful not to let them suspect that I knew the origin of Eric's wounds. Since then, they'd let me alone.

Each evening when I returned to the hotel I found messages of sympathy waiting for me, from people Eric worked with, the Arnellis, Marceline Lafont. . . .

Marceline had received a new passport and was about to return to France. For her, the whole painful episode was over.

I'd also received a letter from my mother but hadn't read it. I'd written her to say that I'd broken my engagement with Philippe, that Eric had suffered a serious accident and that I intended to marry him when he recovered from it. Knowing how she felt about Eric, I was afraid she would reply with vehement reproaches I was in no condition to tolerate, so I kept the sealed envelope in my purse, deciding not to open it till Eric was out of danger.

I waited ten days to read my mother's letter. Maybe I could have done it sooner, since Eric was regaining his strength and the doctors were encouraged by his progress, but somehow I didn't dare assume that his recovery was certain.

One morning as I walked into his room he pointed to a basket of orchids on the table.

"Look at the card that came with those flowers."

I picked up the card and read:

I am happy to learn that you are now convalescing and I hope that you will soon be completely well.

Saad ben Ibrahim Abed

"Is it true?" I asked Eric.

"That Abed sent me flowers?"

"No, that you're considered to be convalescing now."

"Didn't the doctor tell you? Pack your suitcases; we're leaving in a week."

"You're exaggerating!"

"Well, maybe a little, but it won't be long now."

I remembered my mother's letter; now I could read it. I told Eric about it and added, "She's probably written to tell me that she never wants to lay eyes on me again if I marry you."

But when I opened the envelope I saw that she had written only to say she hoped Eric would recover quickly.

"Is it as bad as you thought?" he asked.

"No, it's much better."

I read the letter to him.

"And I was hoping you'd prove your love by breaking off with your family to marry me!" he said, laughing. "By the way, Abed has offered to let me stay in a villa he owns near Homs."

"That won't make up for what he—"

I stopped short. Since we hadn't yet been able to talk for very long at a time, I still wasn't sure how much he knew about his stabbing and I hesitated to

bring up the subject now, for fear of overtiring him.
But the glimmer of amusement in his eyes told me
that he was well aware of what Abed had done.

"You know?" I asked.

"Taoufik told me about your conversation with
Philippe, and before then I already had a pretty good
idea of what had happened. Since I wanted to take
Philippe's place, I suppose I only got what I
deserved, but...."

I put my hand over his lips.

"You mustn't talk too much."

He grasped my hand and held it firmly in his.

"I was going to say that even though I nearly died
because of what I did, I don't regret it. If I had it to do
over again, I'd take the same chance."

"I wish I could say I don't regret anything. I'll
always be sorry it took me so long to discover...."

"The truth, Dina?"

"Yes. I was discouraged because the harder I tried
to find it, the more it seemed to slip away from me.
Yet I really knew it all along."

"I tried to tell you, the day we went to Yeffren."

"I remember."

"Since you had to come to Tripoli to learn that,
have you forgiven me for my ... unusual way of
bringing you here?"

I leaned forward and kissed him. He seemed
satisfied with my answer.

Dear Reader:

We hope you have enjoyed this Mystique Book and are looking forward to future novels in the series.

We would greatly appreciate it if you could help us make Mystique Books even better by answering this questionnaire and returning it to us.

Many thanks for your assistance.

1. Age: under 18 _____
18 – 24 _____
25 – 34 _____
35 – 49 _____
50 or older _____

2. How many paperback books do you usually read a month? _____

3. How many paperback books do you usually buy a month? _____

4. How many Mystique Books have you read so far? _____

5. How would you rate this Mystique Book compared to other paperback you have recently read?

_____ Superior...far better than most
_____ Very good...better than most
_____ Average...no better, no worse
_____ Below average...poor
_____ Very poor...worse than most

6. Would you recommend this Mystique Book to a friend?

_____ Yes _____ No

7. Based on this Mystique Book, would you buy other books in the Mystique series?

_____ Yes...definitely
_____ Probably
_____ Perhaps...not sure
_____ No...not likely

MAIL TO:	Mystique Reader Service MPO Box 707 Niagara Falls, New York U.S.A. 14302	In Canada: Mystique Reader Service Stratford, Ontario N5A 6W2

Name: _____

Address: _____

City/Town: _____ Postal Code: _____

State/Province: _____

HMY 018